CONSTABLE
ALONG THE
HIGHWAY

A perfect feel-good read from one of
Britain's best-loved authors

NICHOLAS RHEA

Constable Nick Mystery Book 24

JOFFE
BOOKS

Revised edition 2021
Joffe Books, London
www.joffebooks.com

First published in Great Britain in 2001
by Robert Hale Limited

ISBN: 978-1-78931-840-1

CHAPTER 1

During a routine patrol around the highways and byways of my picturesque countryside beat, the radio in my Mini-van crackled into life. I responded with 'Delta Alpha Two-Seven receiving' and was rewarded with the unfamiliar Welsh accent of Ashfordly's new sergeant. It sounded strange here because I was more accustomed to the accents and dialects of the North York Moors, but his voice reflected a growing tendency for people to join police forces many miles from their home districts. The days when the North Riding Constabulary comprised officers recruited chiefly from within the county had long gone. We had two Australians within our ranks, and even a sergeant whose place of birth was somewhere in deepest Norfolk — and I must not forget a couple of detectives who had transferred from the London Metropolitan Police to seek a better and more relaxed lifestyle.

'Sergeant Craddock here, PC Rhea. Good morning to you.' Sergeant Blaketon's successor sounded brisk and business-like.

'Good morning, Sergeant,' I responded in a formal manner, for it wasn't often one heard pleasantries among the formalities of official police radio conversations.

'I thought I would come and meet you on your beat, PC Rhea, so you can show me something of the patch for which you are responsible. It is a nice spring morning, so what better introduction could I have?'

'It's very pleasant,' I had to agree. 'What time and where shall we make our rendezvous?'

'I was planning for about an hour's time — say eleven o'clock? Where are you now?'

'Just leaving Elsinby, Sergeant. I've been to High Warren Farm, checking livestock registers and to Sycamore House to renew a firearm certificate.'

'So, eleven o'clock then? You can accommodate me in your busy schedule?'

'No problem, Sergeant, eleven will be fine.'

'Good. And where do you suggest we meet, PC Rhea? How about somewhere that gives me an impression of the expanse of your beat?'

'How about Aidensfield Beacon?' I suggested. 'It gives a panoramic view of the area and you can look across a good deal of my beat, including several of the villages.'

'All right, Aidensfield Beacon it is. And then perhaps you could introduce me to some of your regulars? The landlord of the Brewers' Arms perhaps? Or the Hopbind Inn? But I prefer to keep away from your new postmaster for the moment — I do not want ex-Sergeant Oscar Blaketon telling me how he did my job or how I should do it!'

'Point taken!' I assured him. 'And you can find the Beacon?'

'I do know the roads of the district, PC Rhea, I have climbed that hill up to the Beacon many times on my cycle and I know my way around that part of England for which I am responsible. Till eleven then. Control Out.'

I had met Sergeant Craddock on a few previous occasions; he had recently been posted to Brantsford, a sleepy market town some eight or nine miles away from Ashfordly, having come to that area from a northern division of the county. During the temporary absence of Sergeant Blaketon, whenever he had been enjoying a day off or attending a course, Sergeant Craddock had supervised our work. He had been in the district only a few months, so he was not a complete stranger to me, although I had had comparatively few dealings with him. Nonetheless, his arrival as the officer in charge of the section in which I worked did spark off some interest among the officers of Ashfordly Section. We wondered how he would fit into our cosy rural routine, especially as we had discovered that he and his wife loved ballroom dancing and that he enjoyed touring the countryside on his lightweight cycle. I couldn't imagine him riding his racing cycle in uniform, however, but from a work point of view he was now the sergeant in charge of the combined Ashfordly and Brantsford Sections.

With the advent of better communications and more readily available motor transport, amalgamations of smaller units were inevitable. Craddock would now have responsibility for two market towns — Ashfordly and Brantsford — along with their complement of constables and including a dozen or so village policemen in the surrounding rural areas. I was one of the latter. Craddock's boss was the inspector at Eltering — Eltering was a larger and busier market town with a bigger complement of constables and it also hosted our Sub-Divisional Headquarters. The Divisional Headquarters was at Malton, with a superintendent in charge.

As I patrolled my patch prior to meeting Craddock, I tried to anticipate some of the questions he might ask — he'd want to know my crime rate and my detection figures, he'd want to know if there were any trouble spots like dance halls or badly-run public houses; he'd want to know if any known or suspected criminals lived on my patch or whether I had any accident black-spots which might require the attention of the Accident Prevention Department or the County Highways Officer. And he would want to know a lot more!

I guessed, for example, that he'd ask if there were any important people living on my patch, such as magistrates, Members of Parliament, county councillors, police committee members and others of influence such as the titled estate owners or leaders of the community. In trying to anticipate his approach, I found a quiet layby near Briggsby, parked the van and went through some of the papers in the briefcase which always accompanied me on my patrols around Aidensfield beat. Well before our rendezvous, therefore, I was fully informed of everything which had happened recently on my patch, and aware of all the likely problems which might arise. And so, in due course, I drove up to Aidensfield Beacon to meet my new sergeant.

He had arrived ahead of me. His little black Ford Anglia, immaculately polished, was parked on a patch of ground beside the road on the summit and he was standing with his back to the road, gazing across the seemingly endless view. From that point, it was possible to see a huge heather-covered expanse of the North York Moors to the North and East, along with its range of hills and dales.

Then, if one turned around to face the west, there was the distant panorama of the Yorkshire Dales and the lofty Pennine range some sixty or seventy miles beyond the Vale of York, while to the south were the more gentle summits of the Yorkshire Wolds. And lying in the valleys, or dales as we called them, were green fields, sparkling rivers and scores of pretty villages comprising yellow limestone houses with red pantiles — and a smattering of thatched roofs — all with well-tended gardens. Time and time again, I had admired this astonishing view, and each time I thought I was gazing into Paradise. It was probably a view of this quality which the devil had used to tempt Christ! After all, much of this was my personal kingdom! I eased my Mini-van into a space beside his car and climbed out, leaving the radio switched on.

'Good morning, Sergeant.' I spoke as I approached him from the rear.

'What a wonderful view, PC Rhea, magnificent in fact.' He turned around and smiled. 'You must have the best view of any constable anywhere in the country, you know that? People would pay a fortune to have this aspect from their home, or even enjoy it on holiday, and you have it quite free of charge, almost on your doorstep.'

'When I go to towns like Middlesbrough or some of those in the Midlands, I realise how lucky I am.' I was now at his side. 'This is one of the most under-publicised parts of England; it's Yorkshire's best-kept secret and I hope it remains so!'

'Surely you want to share your joy with those less privileged than you?' he countered. 'I'm from the Welsh valleys, you know, back-to-back houses, coal mines, grime, working-class values and — sometimes when there is no work — extreme poverty. You must never prevent those people from dreaming dreams of living somewhere like this, PC Rhea, or even just paying a visit to such a place. Tourists might be a nuisance, PC Rhea, but they do prevent some rural communities from dying or stagnating. But we are not here to philosophise, we are here to discuss our work as professional police officers. So, where are your beat boundaries? We can get a good idea of most of them from here, can we?'

'Most of them,' I said. I showed him Briggsby on its hilltop site with the spring sun gleaming from the houses, Crampton with its huge stately home on a wonderful riverside site, tiny Ploatby without even a shop or inn, and pretty Elsinby with its castle among the trees, delightful village inn called the Hopbind, and a stream trickling along the side of the village street. Away in the distance, I pointed to the remote Ghylldale in the hills beyond Aidensfield, the quiet Waindale and the equally isolated Lairsbeck hidden in the dale behind Briggsby. Nearer, we could see the huge Benedictine abbey of Maddleskirk in its hillside setting, the waterworks of Lower Keld and the ancient parish church of Thackerston. I could see beyond the boundaries of my own beat, over towards Craydale, Seavham, Falconbridge, Galtreford, Whemmelby and Slemmington, some of which were within the former Brantsford section.

'You will be patrolling some of the places in Brantsford section on a more regular basis, PC Rhea,' he smiled. 'Now that Ashfordly and Brantsford Sections have merged, you will be expected to patrol an expanded area. And likewise, the constables of Brantsford will be patrolling this part of the world. It will be good experience, PC Rhea; you will undertake more work and it will be of a greater variety — and that must be good for any career-minded police officer.'

After I had explained something of my patch to him, he asked me about the crime rate for Aidensfield beat and noted there was one offence which had not been detected.

'It was a travelling car thief, Sergeant,' I explained. 'He took a car from York, dumped it in a farm gate near Elsinby, stole another car from Elsinby and abandoned it in Eltering, took one from there and it was found in Middlesbrough . . . that was two months ago. He left no prints in the vehicles — I can't see we'll ever detect that one.'

'But we shall maintain an everlasting vigil, PC Rhea, shall we not? Our files are never closed. I do not like crimes to remain undetected when a little effort might lead to a successful conclusion.'

'I agree, Sergeant, but apart from that one, all the crimes on my patch have been detected.'

'Very good, PC Rhea, not that many murders, rapes, robberies and arson feature in your figures. It's more like spasms of petty thieving, am I right?'

'Right, Sergeant.'

'And your crime figures are very low, PC Rhea. Only one or two a month, hardly the stuff of villainy, if I may say so. Do you think such a low crime rate justifies a constable working full time in Aidensfield?'

'If there was not a constable working full time here, Sergeant, the crime rate would be higher. The fact I am patrolling on a regular basis, day and night, keeps crime down. Knowing the local bobby is out and about at all hours does persuade the local people to behave themselves, I'm convinced of that.'

'A nice theory, PC Rhea, but one I fear our bosses ignore. If there is little reported crime in an area, they believe it is not worth the expense of a resident constable. And constables are increasingly expensive to maintain these days.'

'If there is no resident constable, there is no one to whom the people can report their crimes,' I countered. 'And if crimes occur but are not reported, it looks as though they are not happening — a false picture is presented. That is aggravated by withdrawing a constable from his patch. The statistics show only a few crimes whereas there could be many which go unreported. Knowledge that crimes are being committed, with no police officers to deal with them, alarms the general public, Sergeant. We should never dispense with our village constables, or any patrolling constables for that matter. They provide both a deterrent and reassurance.'

'There are such things as telephones, PC Rhea! People can summon help and report crimes by telephone, you know.'

'Not everyone has a telephone in these communities, Sergeant, and not everyone lives close to one. And not everyone likes to ring an anonymous place to report a minor crime. They prefer a chat with a constable they know well. Lots of petty crimes are not reported unless the victim happens to come across a patrolling bobby who's got the time for a chat.'

'Quite clearly, you believe a patrolling bobby is important?'

'I do. He is a very reassuring sight for vulnerable members of the public, a sort of insurance.'

'I shall take heed of your concern,' he smiled. 'And now, tell me this. All this land spread out below us like a quilt of many colours — is it all privately owned?'

'Yes, virtually all of it,' I agreed. 'This area is full of large estates, titled people and the gentry, who own the land. They even own some entire villages; parts of my beat are almost feudal. That's why the villages are in such good, clean condition with no dreadful housing estates; the owners don't allow indiscriminate development. Farmers own some of the land too; some own their own farms, some rent them from the estates. Land is important around here.'

'A noble area, Rhea! I must establish a rapport with these people! I must admit I have had very little personal contact with people of quality, PC Rhea. Lords, dukes and the like were not very plentiful in the valleys of Wales where I lived.'

'There's a large concentration of them hereabouts,' I told him. 'The Earl of Sleightholme lives over there—' I pointed to a huge edifice on the skyline — 'and the Duke of Newholme has a house in Elsinby. There's Lord Lexmere in Slemmington; Lord Elterthorpe's estate is on the outskirts of Eltering; the Marquis of Colebeck has a colossal house just down the road from here, and Lord Finedon in that big house on the hillside behind Aidensfield . . . and there's more.'

'So our feudal landowners are still plentiful and powerful, PC Rhea?'

'In a way, yes, but they do maintain standards and provide employment.'

'And they do so while continuing their belief in serfdom, eh? I am one for equality, PC Rhea, something to do with my working-class background, I suspect, and I cannot see why such people can own so much land and exercise so much power . . . but I must not preach: I must learn. I must learn how to work in harmony among these people, for they have rights like anyone else. I must exercise my constabulary duties without fear or favour, am I right?'

'So must we all,' I smiled. 'But I think you will find the estate owners very easy to work with and to understand. For the most part, they are considerate employers and they are very supportive of our work, Sergeant.'

'No tugging forelocks to his lordship and curtsying to the lady of the manor then?'

'Those days have gone, Sergeant,' I assured him.

'I'm pleased to hear it!'

We chatted about my coverage of events like village dances, hunt balls and other public functions where trouble might arise among young people, and he quizzed me on my system of patrolling the villages on my patch. I explained I liked to use the van for travelling between the communities, and then patrol on foot for a time, visiting key venues like the pub, the post office, the shop, the school or other such places to become acquainted with the people. One function of that kind of patrolling was merely to show a uniformed presence, but another purpose was to conduct discreet enquiries into local crimes, national crimes and even possible future crimes!

Getting to know the public and their personalities was very important to a rural constable. At the end of our chat, I was pleased that he seemed quite content with the way I approached my responsibilities.

'Would you like to meet my wife?' I put to him, when it was clear our meeting was about to conclude. 'I'm expected home at twelve-thirty, for lunch, which means we have time to visit the Brewers' Arms — officially, I mean!'

'Yes, good idea. I believe a good supervisory officer should be acquainted with the families of his subordinates. So lead on, PC Rhea. Introduce me to your local landlord too, and then I shall be delighted to meet Mrs Rhea.'

The landlord of the Brewers' Arms was George Ward and when we arrived in our little procession of two police vehicles, the place was busy with the usual lunchtime gathering of farmers and village men. I introduced Sergeant Craddock and the drinkers had a chat and laugh with him, but we could not enjoy a drink with them as we were on duty and in uniform. And so we moved on, with Craddock telling me he was pleased I was so well known and relaxed among such people. He followed me to my police house and parked outside as I turned my van into my drive.

'Am I right in believing the landlord of the Hopbind Inn at Elsinby is also called George Ward?' he puzzled. 'It is not the same man is it, running two establishments?'

'No, Sergeant,' I said. 'They're cousins. There are lots of Wards hereabouts. I got confused when I first came here, but both are very good landlords; they run trouble-free houses and are most co-operative and helpful to me.'

'Then I have learned something today,' he grinned. 'Now, introduce me to your wife and then I must get back to mine. She does like me to be on time for meals, something not always possible in our profession!'

I took Craddock into the lounge of my house rather than the attached police office and introduced him to Mary;

the children were at school and so there was an air of blessed peace about the place. Although she offered him a cup of tea or coffee, he declined. We enjoyed some small talk, with Craddock saying he would like to arrange some kind of social gathering so that he and his wife could meet all the country policemen and their wives. Both Mary and I agreed that such an event would help some of the distant country bobbies to meet one another. In the wild expanse of the North York Moors, one could work for months without encountering a colleague from another station and without ever meeting their wives. As one, we told him we welcomed his initiative. As he was saying his farewell, I heard my office telephone ringing and hurried through to answer it. Craddock, sensing it might be something connected with police work, abandoned his departure and followed me into the office. He listened with rapt attention as I responded. I grabbed a pencil from the desk and prepared to scribble the gist of the message on to my notepad as Craddock came closer to peer over my shoulder.

'This is Gillian Reed,' said the voice. 'I'm the secretary for the Duke of Stockland . . .'

'I know it,' I said. 'In Craydale.'

'Right. Someone's broken into one of our storerooms, they've taken some claret, several crates . . .'

Craddock would not be able to hear my caller's voice, but I was scribbling on my pad. I had written 'Gillian Reed, secretary. Duke of Stockland. Craydale . . . cases of claret stolen.'

As I listened, he was reading my scribbles and then he nudged me. 'I'll go,' he said. 'You stay and have your lunch, PC Rhea.'

I interrupted my caller to turn to him. 'Sergeant?'

'I said I'll go,' he smiled. 'I need to make contact with these people on your beat, PC Rhea.'

'No, I can see to it, Sergeant,' I said.

'No, I insist. Now, where do I find this secretary person? Gillian Reed, isn't it? She'll have all the details?'

'Yes, she's in Craydale, Sergeant, you'll find her at Craydale Lodge, she's secretary to the Duke of Stockland. She often works from home, she's there now. You can't miss her house; it's right next the road junction, near the gates into the estate. Someone's broken into an outside storeroom and stolen some claret . . . but I can go, you know.'

'No, I insist . . .'

'Hello, Mrs Reed?' she was still on the line. 'Sergeant Craddock is here in my office and he will come immediately. He's new to the area and is anxious to meet people on my beat. He'll be there in ten minutes; he'll come direct to your house.'

Craddock was nodding and beaming, and then, even before I had finished my call, he was putting on his cap and rushing out of the office.

'The sergeant is leaving now, Mrs Reed,' I smiled. 'He'll take all the details when he gets there.'

And so, somewhat puzzled by his enthusiasm, I left that little job to Sergeant Craddock as I went to join Mary for lunch. 'So where's your new sergeant gone in such a rush?' she asked, as I washed my hands at the kitchen sink.

'There's been a break-in at the Duke of Stockland,' I said. 'Some wine stolen from an outside storeroom. Mrs Reed rang, she's the secretary. I don't know why he wanted to attend, jobs like that aren't usually for sergeants!'

'It's unusual, isn't it, for a pub to have a secretary?'

'It's more of a country hotel than a pub, it's got eight bedrooms and the owner's a great one for delegating jobs. He sees no reason why he should do all the paperwork when he can be spending time with his customers. And it suits Mrs Reed — a nice spare-time job only a couple of minutes from home. She works from home most of the time. It's certainly a well-run establishment, more upmarket than the average rural pub. The last time I spoke to Charles Newbury, he said she was doing a wonderful job, taking the chores of routine paperwork off his shoulders. Newbury's the landlord but he owns the place too.'

'Well, it was good of Sergeant Craddock to let you have your lunch in peace; come along, it's ready to go on the table.'

It was a couple of hours later when Sergeant Craddock called me on the radio of my van after I had resumed my patrol.

'Rhea,' he said. 'You did not tell me that the Duke of Stockland was a public house.'

'You didn't give me chance, Sergeant . . . why? What did you think it was?' And as I spoke those words I remembered his earlier statement that he wished to cultivate the gentry of the district. 'Oh, I see . . . sorry, Sarge. You didn't think it was the home of a noble gentleman, did you?'

'I'll complete the crime report for you,' he said abruptly. 'And I hope it is the last I hear of this matter! You should have told me I was going to visit a public house, PC Rhea. That was not made clear in the original message. Police officers must be able to impart information with the utmost clarity. I hope you understand that.'

'Yes, Sergeant,' I said meekly.

It wasn't the last he heard of that incident because, a week later, I arrested a local thief who knew those outhouses contained wine which was fit for a duke.

CHAPTER 2

If there was a single non-criminal activity which kept most police officers very busy during the 1960s, it was infringement of the wealth of road traffic legislation. Few drivers could pass through life without breaking one or other of the motoring laws, or rules of the road as they were politely known.

It was extremely easy to commit a minor transgression such as a parking or lighting offence and even the most careful of drivers, after a moment of weakness or inattention, could find themselves charged with a more serious matter such as careless, dangerous or reckless driving. It was the sheer proliferation of motor vehicles that compelled the government to produce a host of statutes and other regulations, all designed to govern the use of motor vehicles upon our roads. I remember counting the rules and regulations at some point in the 1960s and gave up when I reached 3,000. With at least 3,000 possible offences, many of a very minor nature, it was a good or a very lucky driver, who survived without breaching one of them.

The imposition of so many rules and regulations was also bound to affect other road users too, such as cyclists, horse riders and pedestrians. The days when one could amble freely along life's highway and leap out of the way of an oncoming slow-moving contraption had gone for ever; one had now to be aware of risks from all kinds of vehicles, even when setting out upon a very short journey. Oddly enough, some of the older laws, designed for the drivers of horse-drawn coaches, were still in force.

My favourite was under the Highway Act of 1835 which made it illegal for 'any driver of any carriage whatsoever on the highway quitting the same and going on to the other side of the highway fence'. That was before the advent of public toilets!

One snag was that many regulations produced what were known as 'absolute' offences — in other words, it was not necessary to prove that the culprit intended to commit the offence, or even that he knew he was committing it. For example, if a man drove his car on a road after his third-party insurance had expired, he committed an offence. Even if he did not know his insurance certificate had expired, the offence was complete. The same applied if his driving licence had expired. No knowledge of those facts was necessary. As I write now, in the year 2000, a British driving licence remains valid until one reaches one's seventieth birthday, thus eliminating one of the most prevalent of our 1960s motoring offences (and even as I write, new-style driving licences with photographs are being planned). Speeding was another absolute offence — you were either guilty of speeding or you were not, and the fact you did not know you were speeding was of no consequence.

Some specific driving offences were different, however. If you were charged with driving without reasonable consideration for other users of the road, you could plead that you had given those other drivers every consideration and it was open to the court to make a decision based on all the facts and evidence. It was not uncommon for a bench of magistrates to find a person 'not guilty' of careless driving if he produced a clear-cut and sensible defence.

After all, what is careless in one person's opinion is not necessarily careless in the opinion of others. It was during this climate of new traffic regulations that Mr Caspar Justin Netherton found himself before Ashfordly Magistrates' Court charged with riding a pedal cycle, not being a motor vehicle, on a road without due care and attention, or without reasonable consideration for other persons using the road, contrary to Section 10 of the Road Traffic Act, 1960. In his case, the latter portion of this section was used — he was charged with riding his bike without reasonable consideration for other persons using the road, an offence which carried a fine of ten pounds if dealt with by a magistrates' court. Caspar, however, was not the sort of person to capitulate to the authorities because, he argued, he had given every possible consideration to other road users. When the time came for him to appear at court, therefore, he pleaded 'not guilty' in his booming voice.

This was his story. Caspar was a gentleman in his early seventies, unmistakable due to his exceptional appearance. He was about six feet six inches tall, broad of build, with feet needing shoes like dug-out canoes and hands like the proverbial shovels. He boasted a remarkable head of thick, pure white hair which was long and flowing, and he had a huge moustache to complement that hair-style. It flowed from the sides of his face like streams of gossamer, while his face was ruddy with the health of a countryman and his movements were always quick and positive. He habitually wore a thick brown tweed suit with plus-four trousers, heavy green woollen socks and massive brogue shoes, quite often sporting a fresh carnation in his button hole.

As if to match his physique, he had a voice like a foghorn which he was not afraid to use, and it was said he could lift up a recalcitrant youth by the scruff of the neck with just one hand. For this reason, he was regularly asked to be doorman at the hunt ball to keep out the riff-raff, a task at which he was immensely successful. In addition, there was a tale that, in his youth, he had rescued a man from a car which had overturned in a ditch by single-handedly raising the stricken vehicle to allow the much-relieved fellow to clamber to safety.

Caspar lived alone in a wonderfully ornate house on the edge of Aidensfield where he spent much time in his large garden. His wife had died about five years before my arrival as the village constable, but he had four children who lived in various parts of Britain, and they had produced eight or nine grandchildren on whom he doted. He was a kindly, warm fellow who liked a few pints in the Brewers' Arms with a good sing-song to follow if the other regulars were in the mood. If they were not in the mood, he would sing by himself!

When I arrived in Aidensfield, Caspar drove an ancient open-topped Rolls Royce. It was large enough to accommodate his massive frame and most of his grandchildren if they came to visit him, and he would tour the countryside in this splendid vehicle, going off to meet his friends perhaps for a game of golf, salmon fishing in the Highlands or a day's shooting on the North York Moors. Although he looked like a gamekeeper, or even a Scottish laird, he was a retired wine and spirits merchant with friends and contacts throughout the north of England and Scotland. He enjoyed a wonderful life with an equally wonderful lifestyle.

And he was always kind, generous and cheerful — everyone liked Caspar. I had come across him several times in the village but had never been to his house — Juniper Lodge. Then one morning, as I was on one of my routine patrols, I happened to be driving past the entrance to Juniper Lodge and noticed one of his stone gate pillars, the one on the left as I approached from the road, had been demolished. It appeared to have been struck by a heavy vehicle for it now lay in an untidy heap of stones some seven or eight yards from the public road; the other pillar, and the gate itself, were not damaged which suggested the gate had been standing open at the time. As I had not passed that way for a few days, I did not know how recently the damage had occurred. I decided I would inform Caspar, just in case he did not know, and so I turned down his long drive. I wound my way through a tunnel-like canopy of trees to find myself on a gravelled forecourt and when I eased my Mini-van to a halt, Caspar appeared from the side of the house.

'Ah, Constable!' he boomed. 'I thought I heard a vehicle coming. Good of you to call, so what can I get you?'

'Oh, well, I might not be staying . . .'

'Nonsense!' His loud voice rang in my ears. 'It's my coffee time and I do like to share it with someone. Come in, Mrs Clayton will see to it.'

He had not asked the reason for my presence, but I felt it would be acceptable for me to join him for a coffee — it was not as if I was going to book him for an offence! No bribery was intended!

He led me through the front door, into a hallway with a polished wooden floor, Persian rugs and antique furniture, then we turned right into his lounge which looked south over his garden. It was also full of antiques, oil paintings and water colours, with a pair of sumptuous three-piece suites. He opened another door and bellowed, 'Coffee for two please, Mrs Clayton, in the lounge. And biscuits.'

Then he indicated one of the easy chairs. 'Sit down, Mr Rhea.'

As I sank into the upholstery, he smiled and said, 'I like to have callers, Mr Rhea. Life gets a bit on the bleak side when one is all alone. Having a housekeeper is not the same as having a wife; no sense of companionship, if you understand.'

'I can't imagine how it must be,' I smiled. 'I've a house full all the time . . . four children make a lot of noise and stop us getting bored . . .'

'Lucky you! I had that once, a house that was never empty and never quiet, but mine have flown the nest . . . mind, they do come back regularly, usually when they want something! But what can I do for you?'

At that point, Mrs Clayton entered with a tray of coffee and biscuits, and I refrained from making my little speech about his gate pillar.

'Place it on the table, Mrs Clayton, we'll help ourselves. You know PC Rhea from the village?'

His housekeeper, a mousy woman wearing an all-embracing apron and with no smile on her face, nodded and said, 'Hello.' I knew her by sight — she lived in nearby Elsinby — and then she disappeared, closing the door as she left.

Caspar went to the table and poured the coffee, asking if I wanted milk or sugar — I accepted the milk but declined the sugar, and then he placed a couple of chocolate biscuits on a plate and put them on a coffee table before me. I said my thank-yous with great pleasure.

'So, PC Rhea? What can I do for you? Not in some sort of trouble, am I?'

'No, nothing like that.' I was enjoying the coffee. 'I was passing your gate and saw that something has demolished one of the pillars. It's a bit of a mess — it looks as if a lorry or something has hit it. I thought you'd better know — I wasn't sure if you were aware of it.'

'Oh, that's decent of you. But there's no problem: I did it myself.'

'You did?' I must have sounded surprised.

'Ran into it with my old Rolls, at the weekend. Saturday afternoon. I wasn't drunk, I hadn't even been for a drink, in fact I'd been shopping for groceries! At Eltering. And when I turned into the drive, I misjudged the gap and ran slap bang into my gatepost. Damned stupid thing to do, PC Rhea, but entirely my own fault. I don't have to report it to you, do I?'

'No, nothing like that!' I sought to assure him. 'It's on your own private property and you did it yourself anyway — I just thought you ought to be aware of it in case it was a hit-and-run. We might have been able to trace the person who did it, if it hadn't been you. It's all part of the local constabulary service.'

'Well, it's jolly decent of you to bother, but I have contacted a local builder who'll come and fix it; this week all being well, he promised me.'

'I hope he makes a good job of it,' I made a suitable comment.

'Oh, I'm sure he will once he gets started. Mind you, the Aidensfield craftsmen operate on a different time-scale from the rest of us. If you don't ask them which year they're coming to do a job, it could take three or four years to get it done. I've learned that much about local life!'

'Well, it has been said that Yorkshire dialect has no equivalent of *mañana* — we don't have that degree of urgency here!'

'Well, actually, that mishap did make me think, PC Rhea. Between you and me, I've been experiencing a few things like that in recent months. Not seeing other drivers, misjudging distances and openings, being very slow to react when braking, that sort of thing. I'm in decline, I know that and accept it. It's my age.'

'Have you seen a doctor?' I put to him. 'It might be something he can cure.'

'I've been to see him, yes; that argument with my gatepost convinced me I should do something, and my quack says there's nothing he can do. It's all due to the rapidly increasing effect of the ageing process.'

'I'm sorry.'

'So am I, because I've decided to give up driving, Constable. I'm far too much of a risk to be on the road, especially with the speed and volume of modern traffic. I'd be a hazard, I know that. So I've surrendered my driving licence and shall be selling my old Rolls. When I've got the bumper fixed, that is. Mind you, there was not a lot of damage, those old crates are built like tanks. The pillar came off worst!'

'So what will you do? For getting out and about, I mean?'

'My dear wife had a wonderful old bicycle, one of those sit-up-and-beg things with a curved frame and a basket on the front. It's been in one of my sheds for years, ever since she died. It's in perfectly good condition, so I shall use that for local trips, then for longer outings, I shall take a taxi, beg a lift or even catch a bus or train.'

'Well, if I can be of any help, I know the routine of most local people, especially those who regularly go into Ashfordly or Eltering. I'm sure they'd give you a lift.'

'Thanks, Constable. But I shall manage. So if you know anyone who wants to buy a vintage Rolls Royce with a crumpled front bumper and wing, let me know.'

'I will,' I smiled.

'Right, let me show you this old bike. It came from Holland; it's built like a tank as well, but I don't think it's too heavy for me to handle. I think I can manage it even if I am something of a risk at the wheel of a car.'

After coffee, he took me into one of his outbuildings and there was a large bright red cycle, in immaculate condition, with a large basket above the front wheel and a pair of matching red panniers at each side of the rear wheel. He removed it from its parking place near the wall and wheeled it around, saying, 'If you want a good bike, Constable, go to Holland. They make their bikes fit to carry anything from the weekly groceries to a set of gardening tools, by way of extra passengers, dogs and even umbrellas. This is a lady's bike, but it will see me through the rest of my days and it's bright enough for drivers to see me coming and to keep their distance!'

'And, you don't need a driving licence for it!' I smiled.

'My doctor said if I had a medical, it would mean handing in my licence,' he said ruefully. 'So I've avoided that. I hate being told what I can or cannot do, so I have made my own decision. That's why I surrendered my licence — in fact, I sent it yesterday. So I'm grounded now, Constable, except for this red devil of a bike.'

'I think you are a wise man, Mr Netherton.'

'I just like living in peace, Constable,' he smiled ruefully. 'But please call again — you don't need a reason and the coffee will always be on around eleven.'

'Thanks,' I said, and after some inconsequential chatter, I took my leave. Like everyone else, I found myself liking Caspar and felt somewhat sorry for him but accepted that he had done the right thing. He had had the sense to see that he was becoming a risk while driving his car and had done something positive about it. I admired him for that.

During my periodic patrols, I did not catch sight of Caspar on his red bicycle, but local intelligence revealed he had sold the Rolls to a delighted collector and had taken to walking a good deal. From time to time, when I had a few spare moments, I popped in for a chat and a coffee and he seemed to welcome my periodic presence — my world and his were not in the least similar and he liked to hear my stories about police work while I listened to his tales of travel and of big business.

Then, several months after Caspar had decided to abandon driving, I was faced with a problem. It began about six o'clock one Sunday evening when someone knocked on the door of my office. Because I was not on duty — it was a rare weekend off — Mary responded.

This was the system we used, otherwise I would never have a complete day away from work. Unless it was a dire emergency of some kind, she would explain that the constable was not on duty and as she was not able to deal with the matter, the caller should report the problem to Ashfordly Police Station. And that is what happened on that occasion.

'Who was that?' I asked when she returned.

'A motorist,' she told me. 'He said he had a complaint to make about a cyclist.'

'And you told him to go to Ashfordly?'

'He wasn't very pleased about it, in fact he was rather angry and said he was determined to report the matter; he wanted to make an example of the cyclist because he was riding on the wrong side of *the* road. He said it was down-right dangerous, so he said he would go to Ashfordly Police Station in person to report it. I offered to let him use your telephone, but he said he preferred the personal contact.'

'Well, you did the right thing,' I said, and we went outside into the front garden to enjoy the evening sunshine. I did not pursue the matter at that stage, thinking it was not a major problem in which I should concern myself while off duty and enjoying a summer weekend. But next morning, prompt on the stroke of nine o'clock as I was beginning my day's duty, the office telephone rang, and it was Sergeant Craddock.

'Ah, PC Rhea.' His Welsh accent sounded very strong over the phone. 'You had a pleasant weekend, I hope?'

'Very nice, Sergeant, thank you. The weather was good, and it was most enjoyable.'

'Well, I had a call yesterday evening, from a rather irate gentleman who also happens to be a magistrate in Middlesbrough. He said he had called at your house, but you were out — as you are perfectly entitled to be on your rest day. However, he has made a formal complaint about the behaviour of a cyclist on the Aidensfield to Elsinby road, a large and somewhat elderly man in a brown tweed suit and plus fours who was riding a ladies' red cycle — he was facing into the oncoming traffic because he was riding on the wrong side of the road.'

'I'll have a word with him, Sergeant.'

'You know him, then? This cyclist?'

'Yes, I do. That description can only fit one person. I'll pop down to see him this morning. I'm sure there is a perfectly logical explanation.'

'You'll do more than have a word with him, PC Rhea. You will report him for riding a bicycle without reasonable consideration for other users of the road. In fact, his behaviour might even amount to reckless or dangerous cycling, a much more serious offence. I have a written statement from the complainant — you had better peruse it before speaking to your cyclist.'

'I'll come straight away,' I said.

I learned that Sergeant Craddock had interviewed the complainant, a man called James Sneddon, who said he was a railway worker, a trade union official, Labour councillor and magistrate at South Bank, near Middlesbrough.

He had been out for a drive with his wife and while travelling from Elsinby towards Aidensfield, on a B-class road, he had seen a cyclist ahead of him. At that point, he said in his statement, the road is fairly straight for several hundred yards and he had a long and clear view of the approaching cyclist. The cyclist, who was alone, was riding close to the verge, and the complainant saw him ride in that manner for several hundred yards. As he passed the cyclist, Sneddon said he waved his hand and blew his horn in an attempt to attract his attention and to remind the fellow he was on the wrong side of the road, but the man disregarded him and continued to ride his cycle. Sneddon pulled into a convenient gateway and watched the cyclist who continued his journey entirely on the wrong side of the road. Sneddon estimated the cyclist must have covered about half a mile before disappearing around a corner, still on the wrong side of the road. Sneddon did manage to get a very comprehensive description of the cyclist but made no attempt to confront him. He reported the matter to Ashfordly Police Station with a demand that this plus-four-clad country gentleman be traced and prosecuted; he said the country people were not above the law, whoever they were, and added he would be pleased to appear in court as a witness for the prosecution. Sergeant Craddock had then motored out to Aidensfield and Elsinby but had found no sign of the man on the red bike. Now, the matter was my responsibility. I had to report poor old Caspar for this breach of road traffic law, but I must admit I wondered what on earth he had been doing. Perhaps he was more ill than anyone suspected?

It was getting on for 10.30 that Monday morning when I pulled up in front of his house and I found him weeding one of his borders. He straightened up, eased his aching back and came towards me.

'Good timing,' he beamed. 'I was ready for a coffee break.'

'Before you give me coffee, Mr Netherton, I must say I'm here on business. I've had a complaint about you, about your cycling, to be precise.'

'From that foul-mouthed twit who swore at me yesterday evening?' he smiled.

'He said he did not speak to you.'

'Due to his dreadful tongue, I did not listen to him, Constable; he used some profane and dreadful language, the sort one would expect of a dim-witted docker. I never respond to that kind of talk, not even in anger.'

'He's a magistrate on Teesside . . .'

'That doesn't surprise me! So what's his grumble?'

'He wants you prosecuted for cycling on the wrong side of the road,' I said. 'He claims he saw you ride for several hundred yards on the wrong side, between here and Elsinby yesterday evening, and I have to report you for reckless, dangerous or careless cycling. He reported the matter to my Sergeant,' I added for good measure.

Caspar smiled. 'Then let us get on with it, Constable. You take me to court and I will prove I was not being reckless, dangerous or careless. He will be a witness against me, will he not? He'll have to give evidence?'

'Yes, this is his road show!' I laughed.

'And I shall be allowed to cross-examine him?'

'Yes,' I said,

'Good. I shall admit riding my bike at that time but shall plead not guilty to the charge so that he is obliged to attend, and I shall enjoy every moment of it. You'll be there?'

'Yes, I have to attend and give evidence, as the officer who interviewed you.'

'Then all I wish to say to you, officially, is "I plead not guilty". How's that?'

'Perfect,' I said, then I added, 'So why were you riding on the wrong side of the road, Mr Netherton — this is not for the record, by the way, I'm just curious?'

I wondered if he would trust me, but after a moment of consideration he decided he would and said, 'It's far safer, in modern traffic conditions, to ride a cycle while facing oncoming traffic. That's recommended for people *walking* along the road, so why can't the same logic apply to cyclists? A motorist has to ease out to overtake a cyclist who is approached from behind, and he must do the same manoeuvre if the cyclist is facing him. Whether the cyclist is facing a motorist or has his back to him, it makes no difference to the motorist. And if the cyclist is facing oncoming traffic, he can see what is heading towards him. He's not surprised if a vehicle comes up behind without him hearing it, as can happen in windy conditions. In court, I shall maintain I was not riding carelessly — I had given the matter a lot of thought — nor was I dangerous or reckless because I was not doing anything I would not have done at the other side of the road. And, Constable Rhea, you will know this — there is no law to say I should cycle on the left, is there? So I have not committed any offence — and I shall go to court and say so!'

I could understand his logic — certainly, a cyclist who was facing oncoming vehicles had an advantage over one who had his back to the traffic, and his position on the road should make no difference to passing vehicles. They would have to pass him whichever side of the road he was upon, although there might be problems at roundabouts and crossroads! But it was a matter for the learned bench of magistrates at Ashfordly Magistrates' Court at some future date.

In due course, Caspar received a summons for the lesser offence of cycling without reasonable consideration for other users of the road, and he appeared at Ashfordly Magistrates' Court one Friday morning. Sergeant Craddock was prosecuting the case, as was the system at that time, with James Sneddon as his key witness. I was there to give evidence of my interview and the case was marked as No. 7 on that morning's court sheet. Eventually, it was our turn. Sergeant Craddock outlined the case in much the same way that Sneddon had provided his account of the incident, and he rounded off his presentation by saying that, in riding towards oncoming traffic, the defendant had been cycling without reasonable consideration for other users of the road. I gave my evidence — all I could say was that I had interviewed the defendant about the alleged offence whereon he had admitted riding his cycle at the place and time in question, and that he had stated his intention to plead 'not guilty' to the offence. I did not say I had listened to Caspar's explanation — that had not been part of my interview.

Craddock then called his star witness — James Sneddon, his foul-mouthed complainant.

He provided a lurid account of his experience, saying he had been shocked to find an elderly gentleman on a lady's cycle heading towards him on the wrong side of the road and as he gave his evidence, I watched the body language of the magistrates. I sensed they did not like this rather strident townie magistrate, and eventually it was Caspar's turn to question this witness.

'Mr Sneddon,' he began in his loud, warm voice, 'I was brought up to be considerate to everyone, irrespective of class, creed or colour, and as a child I was told always to walk facing the traffic if I was on a country road with no footpaths at either side. You will recall that the Elsinby to Aidensfield road has no such footpaths. But I was not walking, I was riding my cycle — I have admitted that. You saw me, I believe?'

'Of course I saw you, that's why we are here!'

'Did you come upon me suddenly?'

'No, I had a long view. I saw you ahead of me and I could not believe it . . . a grown man cycling on the wrong side of the road . . .'

'A long view? How long a view, Mr Sneddon?'

'Several hundred yards, you rode for almost half a mile that I could see.'

'Without mishap?'

'Well, yes, there was no trouble.'

'And the road is a B-class, I believe? Wide enough for two vehicles to pass with ease, two large vehicles, in fact.'

'That is not the point—'

'Can two vehicles pass easily?' persisted Caspar.

'Yes, they can!'

'So the action of overtaking a lone cyclist is not fraught with danger on that road, whichever side he happens to be on?'

'Well no, I was not in any danger . . .'

'And neither was I, was I? You were driving in a perfectly normal manner?'

'You were not in any danger, no. I am a good driver, I pride myself on my driving,' agreed Sneddon.

'And would you say that I cycled with every consideration for you? I was riding on my nearside, as close as possible to the verge, with both hands on the handlebars and not riding at speed or in a reckless or dangerous manner.'

'No, there was nothing wrong with the way you were cycling, it was just the fact you were on the wrong side of the road, facing the traffic.'

'Nothing wrong with the way I was cycling? Thank you, Mr Sneddon,' and Caspar now addressed the bench. 'I am not charged with riding on the wrong side of the road, Your Worships,' he smiled. 'There is no such offence in road traffic law. And even this witness — this only witness — says I was not being careless or dangerous or reckless. How then can I be guilty of cycling without reasonable consideration to other users of the road? I gave all users of that road every possible consideration, that is precisely the reason I cycled in the face of oncoming traffic. It is far safer than riding with one's back to the traffic.'

And he sat down.

He was not called to give evidence — he'd made all his points in his cross-examination of the witness, and the magistrates went into a huddle. After some hushed whispers, the chairman of the bench indicated a decision had been reached, and he called Caspar to stand before them.

'Caspar Netherton,' he said, 'we have listened to the evidence and although your actions were unconventional, we find no evidence to prove you were riding a bicycle without reasonable consideration for other road users. Indeed, you seem to have given them every consideration. And, as you rightly say, there is no offence of riding on the incorrect side of the road. The case is dismissed.'

Afterwards, I wondered if this gave *carte blanche* for every cyclist to ride along the wrong side of the road into oncoming traffic, but the case did not create much of a fuss in the newspapers or legal journals. Although most other cyclists continued to ride with their backs to the traffic, Caspar Netherton always rode his cycle while facing oncoming traffic and he was never involved in an accident, nor were there any other complaints about his conduct. And I continued to visit him — after all, he did make rather nice coffee.

* * *

One of the problems with children is that they listen intently to adult conversations and then translate everything quite literally. Young Stephen Bailey, aged eight, was such a boy, and it was perhaps unfortunate that his father, Bernard, tended to speak in clichés or even proverbs. He did this at home, at work and when he was socialising in the village, usually at the Brewers' Arms.

He continued his unique style in most other forms of general conversation and, of course, his children overheard this curious way of conducting a conversation. At times, I felt he required a translator. For example, instead of saying he didn't want to cause a fuss, Bernard would say 'I don't want to upset the apple cart', at which young Stephen would wonder which apple cart his dad was talking about. Once, he searched the village for his dad's apple cart. The child also had problems with 'I've no axe to grind'. Because he overheard that statement from dad, he once asked his mum to buy his father an axe for his birthday, presumably so he could grind it; while 'I don't want to teach my grandmother to suck eggs' created a wonderful mental picture in Stephen's young mind, especially as Bernard did not have a grandmother. She had died some years earlier.

As the village constable, I often wondered where Bernard had found his apparently unlimited stock of such sayings — everything he did was shipshape and Bristol fashion, he was always waiting until his boat came in, his money did not grow on trees, he often pulled out all the stops as he lived on a shoestring after sometimes being sold down the river. The proof of all his puddings was in the eating, although he often said he could not live by bread alone, but two heads were better than one while the devil was not as black as he was painted, and every cloud had a silver lining. Necessity was the mother of invention, an ill wind did no one any good and whenever he was temporarily out of work or seeking a contract, Bernard would say, 'Well, it's time I got on my bike!'

Bernard was an honest, genuine man in his mid-thirties who had three small children and a very supportive wife called Maureen. Of stocky build and balding, with a round, happy face, he ran a battered old Ford Cortina and an equally battered pickup truck. With a neat stone house at the west end of the village, he was a good-humoured, self-employed builder who earned most of his money from repairs and alterations to existing properties. He was a good craftsman, that was never in doubt, but, sometimes, he found it difficult to find work while at other times he was inundated with commissions. But he made a reasonable living, sometimes having lots of money to spend, and at other times relying on the kindness of his local bank manager to see him through a crisis. If anything was in his favour, it was that he was trustworthy and reliable; his work was skilled, and he never took advantage of the gullibility of some of his customers. In fact, there were times he did work for nothing if he felt his customer could not pay, like some pensioners who needed tiles replacing or walls repointing. In short, everyone in Aidensfield liked Bernard and would help him in any way they could.

One of his strengths was that he never worked on a Sunday. That was the one day in the week he gave to his family, often taking Maureen and the children for an outing in his old car. He would take them to a stream high on the moors where they could play in safety, or he would suggest a picnic at the seaside or a trip to the zoo. It was during one of these trips that Maureen suggested they should get a dog; she felt the children should learn to care for animals and a dog seemed a good idea. They could take it out for walks on the moors.

She was thinking of something small, like a spaniel, a dog which could live in the house and one which would be friendly and tolerant of children. Soon after this notion, and before they'd actually obtained a dog, Maureen was walking in the village street one Saturday morning with Stephen and her two other children, John aged six and Louise aged four. She spotted me, hailed me and asked, 'Nick, the police get stray dogs in, don't they?'

'We do,' I confirmed. 'Lost dogs, wandering dogs, dogs cast away by their owners, unwanted Christmas presents . . . we get them all.'

'So what do you do with them?' was her next question, as Stephen listened intently. 'The reason I'm asking is that we're thinking of getting a dog, and it would be nice to give an abandoned one a good home.'

'We keep ours for seven days,' I said, 'and if they're not claimed, we offer them to that lady in Lairsbeck, the one who keeps the kennels. Lairsbeck Kennels, it's called. You can't miss it, the first house over the stream as you go in from this direction. Mrs Collins — Lucy. She's always there, seven days a week. She takes all our strays and usually finds good homes for them. I'd go and see her if I were you, she gets them in from all over, not just from us.'

'Right, thanks,' she smiled. 'I'll tell Bernard,' and, with her little family, she continued her way to the shop.

Perhaps, at this point, I should mention another one of Bernard's sayings: whenever he went out for a drink to the pub, and the children asked where he was going, he would reply, 'I'm going to see a man about a dog'.

He would often use that phrase too, if he was going on some other mission about which they were too curious. It was his way of doing anonymous things. It was against this background, and very soon after her chat about the dog, that I received a frantic telephone call from Maureen one Sunday lunchtime. It was approaching one o'clock.

'Nick,' she panted into the telephone, 'Stephen's vanished, gone, just like that. I've looked everywhere . . .'

'I'll be there in two minutes,' I said, grabbing my hat and rushing off with a cry to Mary to leave the beef in the oven and delay production of the Yorkshire puddings. I hoped I would not be long. When I got to Bernard and Maureen's house, Bernard had been recalled from his Sunday lunchtime pint and the expressions on their faces showed their acute anxiety.

'I just don't know what to do . . .' Maureen was weeping, and Bernard put a reassuring arm around her shoulder. 'He was in the garden playing with the others, he's always done that, he's never gone off before, and I was getting lunch ready . . . John said he hasn't seen him for a long time. He said Stephen went off on his bike.'

'We got it for his birthday,' Bernard said. 'A two-wheeler. A blue one with white tyres. He's very sensible and rides it well.'

'It's not around then, the bike?' I asked.

'No,' and Maureen shook her head as she burst into another flood of tears.

'I need to search the garden and outbuildings,' I said, 'for Stephen or the bike . . . and I need to talk to John . . .'

Working as quickly as I could, I searched the entire house, including the bedrooms and attic, then all the outbuildings, and quizzed the other two children, and concluded that Stephen had indeed ridden away on his bike.

In trying to determine the time of his disappearance, I learned that Bernard had intended to pay his usual visit to the Brewers' Arms when it opened at twelve noon (Sunday opening hours), but in fact he had left home just after eleven because he wanted to talk business with a man who had bought an old cottage on the outskirts of the village. He'd heard the man was thinking of adding an extension to the ground floor and wanted to offer his services. At that time, all the children had been playing contentedly in the garden as they always did on a fine day when dad was not taking them for an outing; Maureen was in the kitchen preparing lunch and, hearing the noise of children at play, she'd not noticed Stephen's absence.

I obtained a description of Stephen — aged eight, fair hair, blue eyes, medium build for his age, dressed in a blue T-shirt, grey shorts and blue sandals. He was riding a child's bicycle, blue colour with white tyres. And he'd been on the road for almost two hours. How far could a child of that age ride in two hours, I wondered? Five or six miles? I hoped no one had given him a lift.

I radioed Ashfordly Police Station from my Mini-van and suggested that we circulate a description of Stephen and his bike, so that all mobile patrols within the area, including those from the Road Traffic Division, could remain alert to the likelihood of tracing him. Meanwhile, I would scour the village and ask everyone I could find whether they had noticed little Stephen on his travels.

Then I would have to make my own tour of the district — and I hoped nothing awful had befallen him. Fortunately, I found a woman who'd been looking out of her bedroom window soon after eleven and she'd seen Stephen pedalling past on his bike, all alone. He'd been heading East, she said. I told Bernard and invited him to join me in the van as I tried to determine his route — I asked Maureen to remain at home in case Stephen returned, or in case there were any other phone calls or sightings. I raced along the lanes but soon reached a junction — with no sign of Stephen. I reckoned he would have reached this point after twenty minutes normal riding, which meant he could now be a few miles along either of these lanes. I eased to a halt before deciding which route to take.

Then Bernard said, 'I wonder if he's gone to Lairsbeck?'

'Lairsbeck?' I puzzled.

'He's always ear-wigging, Mr Rhea, listening to conversations between me and Maureen. We've talked about getting a dog, you see, from the kennels at Lairsbeck. I know Maureen discussed that with you, Stephen told me. He's been wanting us to go over to Lairsbeck to look at some dogs . . .'

'Bernard, another thing comes to mind! When you were getting ready to go out to the pub, did you say you were going to see a man about a dog?'

'Why would I say that?'

'You always say that when you're going out to the pub!' I laughed.

'Do I?'

'You do. And it wouldn't surprise me if you said you were getting on your bike before you saw that man about his building extension . . .'

'You mean Stephen thought I'd got on my bike to go and see a man about a dog?'

'If you did say that, it might be exactly what he's done!' I chuckled. 'Come along, Bernard. Lairsbeck, here we come.'

We drove along the road to Lairsbeck and sure enough, within a few minutes we came upon little Stephen pedalling like fury as he tried to catch up to the father he thought was somewhere ahead. I drew the van to a halt and said, 'Don't tell him off, Bernard, be gentle with him.'

'Stephen, where are you going?' Bernard asked, as the little chap stopped at the side of the road.

'I thought you'd gone to see a man about a dog,' he said. 'You said you were going to see a man about a dog and you were going to get on your bike, so I thought I'd go as well, to make sure we got a nice dog.'

'I think your mum would like to see the dog as well,' I interrupted. 'Shall we go back and get her? And for now, you can put your bike in the back of my van.'

And so we did that. With the little blue bike rattling in the back of my van, I radioed Ashfordly Police Station to cancel the search and to report the finding of Stephen Bailey safe and sound, then I drove back to Aidensfield with my charges. Bernard said he would take the family to the kennels that very afternoon to look at some dogs, but as I pulled up outside his home, there was another car in the drive.

'Oh, crumbs! The in-laws have turned up!' he groaned. 'It never rains but it pours!'

'It's not raining, is it, Dad?' asked Stephen.

CHAPTER 3

One of the most regular events dealt with by any rural constable during the 1960s was the road traffic accident. If anything could be described as part of a country policeman's
routine, then this was it, because most accidents involving
motor vehicles were reported to the constabulary. There were
a few instances when such reports did not have to be made,
such as running off the road and damaging nothing else but
one's own vehicle, or an incident which caused injury only
to the driver. Similarly, if a minor bump occurred and the
drivers involved exchanged names and addresses, they were
not obliged to report the matter to the police.

Generally, however, if, owing to the presence of a motor
vehicle on a road, an accident occurred whereby personal
injury was caused to a person other than the driver of that
motor vehicle, or damage was caused to a vehicle other than
that motor vehicle, then the driver had to stop, exchange
names and addresses and provide the identification number of the offending car. If such names and addresses were
not exchanged for whatever reason, then the drivers had to
report the matter to the police within twenty-four hours. In
fact, most accidents were reported to us because the offending drivers usually blamed one another and wanted a police

investigation so that their insurance companies would have the necessary data in order to deal with the matter and apportion blame. The general rules also applied to certain animals which were injured by motor vehicles, i.e. dogs, goats, cattle, horses, asses, mules, pigs and sheep but not cats, hens, deer, badgers, foxes, pheasants, elephants or any other animal not specifically mentioned.

In simple terms, if a motor vehicle collided with a black dog and it suffered an injury, then the accident had to be reported, but if one ran into a flock of hens and slaughtered the lot, then it was not necessary to make an official report to the police.

In recording traffic accidents, there was an important road safety aspect. Every reported accident was logged on a large-scale map in the Accident Prevention Department at police headquarters. There was a colour-coded system, using pins with different coloured heads, or miniature flags, and so, at a glance, it was possible to identify all those accidents which were fatal, serious or slight, all which involved pedestrians, cyclists or horse riders, all which involved pedal cycles or motor bikes, cars or lorries, with or without caravans or other trailers. That map contained a mass of information about every accident within the county, but, most importantly, it identified places where accidents repeatedly occurred. The term 'accident black spot' might well have been coined because such a map would have an unwelcome group of pins with black heads, all clustered at one location, if it was regularly the scene of fatalities. Similarly, a cluster of red pins might indicate a place where serious accidents happened on frequent occasions.

This information was subsequently relayed to either the Home Office or the County Highways Department so that any black spot or scene of repeated crashes could be examined with a view to making it a less dangerous place. If accidents did happen frequently at a particular location, it suggested the road or perhaps the design of a junction, crossroads or other feature was at fault rather than a succession of inattentive drivers.

Certainly, many accidents were due to driver error, but the roads themselves contributed to a considerable degree. The system of recording road accidents meant that such problems upon the highways could be identified and as a consequence therefore, roads were straightened out or widened, crossroads were redesigned to give better visibility, blind spots were eliminated, traffic lights and pedestrian crossings installed, road surfaces improved, and narrow bridges widened. If there was a contributory factor to a series of traffic accidents, it would be recognised and dealt with.

From time to time, however, accidents happened due to other factors and not all were reported to the police. On the outskirts of Briggsby, for example, a number of motor cyclists came to grief outside Hill Top Farm because one of the farm dogs, a black and white cur called Rover, had a propensity for chasing motor cycles and trying to bite the ankles of the riders. He would hear the bike approaching long before it reached the vicinity of the farm and would lie in ambush behind a large oak tree. As the bike passed by, Rover would race from his hiding place, snarling and barking as he attempted to seize the nearest ankle. More often than not, the startled motor cyclist would lash out with his foot in the hope it might connect with the dog in a manner which would deter it from repeating this behaviour, but inevitably the kick missed, and the actions caused the bike to wobble and swerve off the road. Fortunately, there was a strategically placed haystack and many of the riders found themselves lying among the thick hay spread around its base and being guarded by the same black and white dog which was now wagging its tail in undisguised joy.

Happily, no injuries occurred during this short-lived sequence of events but when I heard about it, I warned Rover's owner that if Rover persisted in his antics, a court appearance was inevitable. That could result in an order for Rover to be destroyed or kept under control — and so the dog was given to the farmer's son who lived on his own farm in the middle of the moors well away from passing motor bikes. So far as I know, none of those incidents was recorded on the map at police headquarters, although I later heard that Rover had taken to chasing tractors and milk lorries, but — happily for me — not on public roads.

If the haystack outside Hill Top Farm was a temporary accident blackspot so far as Aidensfield rural beat was concerned, then so was a clump of elderberry bushes on the side of the road between Crampton and Lower Keld. For some inexplicable reason one summer, car drivers began to run off the road while negotiating a long and not very acute corner on this wide and hitherto accident-free lane. The first was a fire extinguisher salesman whose company car left the road under mysterious circumstances around eleven o'clock one Wednesday morning. He had driven right off the road and had terminated that trip with his bonnet buried among the branches of the elderberry and his front wheels in a ditch. Had he not been halted by the elderberry bushes or the ditch, he might have continued into a small shallow stream which flowed behind it.

I was called to the scene by an elderly lady, Mrs Ada Newcombe, who lived at Field House, a substantial property which stood on that corner — in fact, that house gave its name to the bend — Field House Corner.

Mrs Newcombe lived with her son and his wife at Field House and was reading in her own ground-floor room when the accident happened. She rang me and so I drove there immediately. I arrived about twenty-five minutes later to find the car driver, a smart-suited individual in his mid-thirties, having a cup of coffee in the kitchen of Field House, and being ministered to by both Mrs Newcombe senior, and her daughter-in-law, Helen. Helen, a good-looking blonde in her early forties, was fabulously dressed and she apologised for having to dash away — she was the newly elected president of Ashfordly Ladies' Luncheon Club and was rushing off to this Wednesday's event to make sure everything was ready for her members and the incoming guest speaker. Mrs Newcombe senior would look after us.

I remained and joined the coffee party in the kitchen, which now comprised the older Mrs Newcombe, the driver and myself. I think we provided a spot of excitement in Mrs Newcombe's rather quiet existence. I discovered the driver was called Alan Kenton who lived in Scarborough, and he could provide no explanation for running off the road. Although he was not obliged to report the accident, there being no injuries to anyone but himself and no damage to another vehicle, the fact I had been called to deal with it meant I had to make the necessary report. I made a note of the incident, drew a sketch plan of the scene, and arranged for a neighbouring farmer to haul the car from the ditch with his tractor. Apart from a few scratches and a broken headlamp glass, it was not seriously damaged. I checked the tyres, but none was punctured, and then I tried the steering; it seemed efficient and I could not identify any other obvious fault with the car.

Kenton had not been drinking and assured me he had not suffered a blackout or fallen asleep. I could ascertain no reason why he should have driven off the road. In such cases, there is always the possibility of charging a motorist with careless driving, the reasoning being that he must have been careless to some degree to have run off the road, but as no other person was involved and no damage had occurred, the decision was invariably not to proceed with a prosecution. And so, after that unexpected interruption to his daily routine, Kenton continued his journey, albeit with a less-than-smart vehicle.

Just over a fortnight later, on a Friday morning, I was patrolling along that same road and came upon a battered-looking man emerging from the stream behind that self-same clump of elderberry bushes. I stopped and then realised his Ford Anglia had run off the road, missed the bushes and concluded its journey nose first into the water. Fortunately, the stream was very shallow, and he suffered nothing more than a soaking to his trousers, socks and shoes, and a few bumps to his head. There was no one else in the car. On this occasion, the man was Gerry Milburn, a plumber in his forties who lived in Crampton, and he was on his way to Ashfordly to visit the dentist. As I dealt with the incident, Helen Newcombe, in a smart suit with a rather short skirt and elegant high-heeled shoes, emerged from Field House and asked if I needed help. I thanked her and declined, then she apologised and said she was rushing off to a hair appointment. As before, I summoned the friendly local farmer who hauled Gerry's car out with his tractor. He was relieved to find it was suffering little damage.

As I'd done before, I checked this one and found no punctures, no steering defects and nothing to indicate why it should have suddenly veered off the road — and Gerry could not help. He just shook his head when I put the question to him. Again, I had to record the incident because I had attended to it.

After I had submitted my report, Sergeant Craddock rang me.

'PC Rhea,' he said. 'Two accidents in such a short time at one location does suggest some kind of problem. Would you say the Accident Prevention Department should examine that road, and Field House Corner in particular?'

'I don't think it's necessary,' I had to say. 'The road has not been altered, there are no changes to the design or the camber of the corner; no new buildings or anything . . . and it's been accident-free since I came here.'

'So these are just a couple of coincidences, you think?'

'There's no other explanation, Sergeant. And neither of them reported swerving to avoid a black dog!'

'Ah, the good old black dog syndrome! How many accidents have been caused by people swerving to avoid fictitious black dogs, I wonder? But there is some kind of mystery here, PC Rhea, so keep an eye on the place. Whenever you travel that way, look out for likely causes of those accidents; you never know, you might just come across something.'

I did so. I was as curious as he to find a reason for this sudden crop of minor accidents on a road which had hitherto been completely safe and so I made a point of using that route as often as possible, at various times of the day.

Each time, however, I found no reason for the spills. One thing I did notice, though, was that the verge between the road and the clump of elderberry bushes bore signs of other vehicles having run off the road. There were several tyre marks, some fairly fresh, and I reasoned these had been made by cars which had run a few feet off the highway without colliding with the elderberry bushes. They had come to rest before impact and had then reversed away. It wasn't a case of over-shooting the corner because they'd all run off on the inward curve.

Then, as if to compound my lack of success, the next accident occurred a month after the first. This time two young men on holiday in the district ran off the road in their open-topped MG and came to rest in the elderberry clump. As before, Mrs Newcombe senior had seen the accident from her downstairs room, rang me and then rushed out to see what she could do. By the time I arrived, she and her daughter-in-law, once again in her finery, were giving each of the shaken youngsters a cup of coffee. As before, Helen apologised for rushing off to her luncheon club while I quizzed the lads — but they said they had no idea why they'd run off the road. The driver, Jonathan Fleming who was twenty-three, just shook his head and could offer no explanation — he'd not been drinking; he'd not fallen asleep; the car tyres were not punctured, and the steering was in good condition. His friend, Andrew Ellis, said he had no idea what had caused the accident, but I detected the merest hint of knowing glances which passed between the pair. I felt they were concealing some information, and I knew that if Jonathan admitted he had been distracted to the extent of running off the road, he was virtually admitting careless driving.

So he said nothing.

When I submitted that report, Sergeant Craddock decided he should accompany me upon a drive along that road. We would use his official Ford Anglia and we would drive from Crampton to Lower Keld with particular emphasis upon the situation at Field House Corner. He said we would do so next Thursday morning. That gave me a few more days to try and find a reason for these accidents.

There was not a lot of data to study; three reported accidents was not many, but all the offending vehicles were cars — no lorries, buses or motor cycles had been involved. Remembering the marks on the verge, they seemed like car tyre marks too, not lorries or heavy vehicles. The accidents had all been during the morning too, in good conditions with clear visibility. Fog or bad weather could not be blamed. None of the drivers had given any clue to the reason for their off-road experience, perhaps wisely remaining silent in view of any likely prosecution if they admitted some act of carelessness. The cars had all been travelling the same direction, i.e. from Crampton towards Lower Keld, and they'd all gone off the road at the same place, some hitting the elderberry bushes and one just missing them. And those bushes were directly opposite Field House.

And then I realised something: on each occasion, Helen — the glamorous blonde — had been rushing off to some function, invariably dressed up to the proverbial eyeballs in her finery. Was that relevant? The tiniest piece of enlightenment began to creep into my mind and I decided to pay another visit to Field House Corner.

Before doing so, however, I made some discreet enquiries and discovered that, on Wednesday next, there was to be racing at York Knavesmire and Helen, with her husband, would be attending. Her luncheon club meetings were once a month, so the dates would not conflict. In my earlier dealings with Helen at Field House, her husband had been absent — he owned a chain of greengrocery shops in the area. His major interest was horse racing and he attended every meeting at York. My enquiries also revealed he and Helen were expected to arrive at noon for lunch at the course prior to the first race; they'd be joining a group of friends for a lively day out. I reckoned they'd be leaving Field House just after eleven, and so I decided to drive down to Crampton that Saturday morning, and make the return trip towards Field House. I would park in a farm gateway just before reaching Field House Corner.

While sitting in the driving seat, I could look along the lane towards Field House and I had a good, clear and open view of the premises. I could see the gentle bend in the road as it ran past the house, and I could see the ill-fated elderberry bushes, now looking somewhat battered and broken. I checked my watch. It was 10.15. I was happy to sit here until the Newcombes departed and the time allowed me to study the house which stood proud and solid ahead of me. Built of local stone, it was a large square structure with three ground-floor windows facing my direction; they overlooked an open field which lay behind a hedge on the opposite side of the road to where I was parked. Upstairs, however, the bedroom windows did not overlook the same field. The front windows looked over the road and the rear ones had views across the fields behind, down towards a distant wood.

But one huge upstairs window faced me. It extended the complete height of the upper floor and comprised large square panes of clear glass, about a dozen in all, and it was clearly at the top of the stairs. A landing window, in other words, which provided light for the central corridor upstairs — all the bedrooms and bathroom would lead from that landing. And then I saw a vision of loveliness! Helen Newcombe, without a stitch of clothing . . . she was hunting through a wardrobe . . .

A car raced past me. It was a large Vauxhall Velox — I recognised it as Rudolph Burley's vehicle; he was our local auctioneer and I guessed he was heading for a farm sale or a house sale somewhere. Then Rudolph's car was bouncing over the grass verge before coming to a noisy standstill in the middle of the elderberry bushes. Helen had now vanished and so I rushed from my van and ran towards Rudolph who was sitting in his seat with a dazed expression on his face. I opened his door and tried to help him out, but he was a large man and I could not budge him, but he appeared to rally and suddenly began to struggle from the vehicle.

At this point, one of the ground-floor windows in the house was opened and old Mrs Newcombe said, 'The coffee's on, Mr Rhea, and you can bring your friend!'

As I helped Rudolph out of his car, with its radiator hissing ominously, I realised the front was damaged. I edged him away and said, 'Come along, Rudolph, away from the car. Are you injured? Bleeding?'

'No, no, I'm all right,' he muttered. 'A bit shaken but all right . . .'

'You need to sit down with a hot drink,' I said. 'Coffee's on across the road. Come along.'

'What about the car?'

'We'll see to that soon, you're more important at the moment.'

I persuaded him to leave his car and escorted him across the road where old Mrs Newcombe had come to the kitchen door. She was holding it open with a big smile on her face, saying, 'This is becoming quite a habit, Mr Rhea, all these gentlemen calling for coffee . . . I really quite enjoy it, you know.'

'Is Helen in?' I asked, just to be sure I had not seen a ghost.

'She's upstairs, getting ready for York Races. Geoffrey's taking her. She does enjoy a day at the races. She'll be down in a minute or two.'

'Thanks, now this is Rudolph Burley, our auctioneer. How are you now, Rudolph?' I asked as he settled on a kitchen chair.

'All right,' he nodded vigorously. 'Yes, all right. No broken bones, a bit shaken . . . what about the car?'

'We have a ready-made system for rescuing cars from that elderberry clump,' I said. 'Jack Nealson, next door. I'll give him a ring and he'll drag your car out, then we can have a look at it. Now, why did you run off the road, Rudolph?'

'Search me,' he shrugged his broad shoulders. 'I don't know what happened.'

'You've not been drinking? Brakes all right? No steering faults?'

'No, nothing like that, nothing . . . I don't know, Nick . . . look, I'm fine and I'd better be going, I've an appointment . . .'

'It sounds as if you've a burst radiator,' I warned him. 'We'd better check it before you set off.'

'I'll ring Jack,' offered old Mrs Newcombe. 'I know he's around, I saw him earlier on his tractor.'

While Mrs Newcombe went off to ring for help, I said, 'I saw what distracted you, Rudolph. We've had a few accidents here in recent weeks, and we didn't know what was causing them. Now I know. Mrs Newcombe, Helen. Upstairs without a stitch on! There's no wonder those other chaps didn't want to talk about it — I'll bet they don't want their wives to know!'

'You won't tell my wife, will you? She'd not be best pleased . . . thinking of me ogling another woman!'

'I won't tell her, Rudolph, but you've got the job of explaining why you ran off the road in the middle of the day in good weather!'

'I'll blame a dog or something. But when that sort of thing happens, you can't help looking, can you? Gut reaction, it was. God, Nick, but what a surprise . . . I mean, you don't expect that sort of thing in a country lane on a Saturday morning, do you? And she is a good-looker, isn't she?'

'She is, and you're not the first; there's been a few chaps in that elderberry bush. I wonder if you'll be the last. Ah, Helen!'

At that point, Helen, dressed in her finery, came into the kitchen closely followed by her mother-in-law. I don't think Helen heard us discussing her bountiful merits because she was chatting loudly. As they entered the kitchen, Mrs Newcombe senior said, 'The tractor is coming, Mr Burley, but you've time for a coffee.'

'Another accident, Mr Rhea?' smiled Helen. 'And I have to rush off again, we're going to the races. Ada will look after you. I'm so glad you're not hurt, Mr Burley. I suppose we should be glad those bushes are there, they're quite a soft landing and they do stop cars going into the stream on that bend . . .'

'Helen,' I said. 'Can I have a word? Very quickly — and privately?'

'Good heavens, Mr Rhea, this sounds very serious!' She led me into the lounge just as her husband came downstairs. He spotted me, and I could see the question-mark in his mind, so I invited him to join us.

Geoffrey, a large and cheerful man, said, 'Can't it wait, Constable, we're off to York for the races? Time's getting on.'

'One minute of your time,' I smiled. 'These accidents that keep happening outside your house . . . er, Helen, it's you I need to talk to.'

'Me?' she sounded surprised.

'This is not easy,' I began, looking at Geoffrey for support. 'But, Helen, when you are preparing to go out for the day, like today, you manage to put yourself in full view of drivers coming from Crampton . . .'

She blushed furiously. 'No I don't, Constable! How can I? My bedroom's at the other side of the house, and the bathroom's in the middle . . . and I do take care . . .'

'Those mirrors, darling,' and I saw the beginning of a smile on Geoffrey's face. 'Perhaps you have forgotten the mirrors . . .'

'Oh my God!' She put her hands to her face, now crimson red with the most delightful blushes. 'You mean all those people will have seen me . . .'

'Only those that crashed, I suspect,' I laughed. 'There's no doubt something distracted them and this morning, when I was out there, I saw you — and so did Rudolph. Luckily, I was stationary, but he went into the elderberry tree, like the others. Whatever he saw, it took his mind off his driving for just an instant. But it was long enough to come to grief!'

'Well, I'm delighted my wife has such an impact on lusty human males!' chortled Geoffrey. 'But come upstairs,

Constable, let's have a look at those mirrors. It might explain things.'

'Oh, this is so embarrassing,' Helen was saying. 'I don't know how I can face those people now . . .'

'It's not your face they'll remember, darling,' chuckled Geoffrey, leading the way.

At the top of the large staircase, the landing was huge, and it ran right through the centre of the house. The window facing the Crampton direction, the one I had seen, was not bearing any net curtains. Geoffrey showed me the bathroom, the bedrooms, and then we turned our attention to the mirrors. Bolted to the walls at intervals along each side of the landing were several huge mirrors, reaching from floor to ceiling and each some four feet wide. One of them was on the wall adjoining the landing window — and that's where I'd seen Helen. In fact, I'd not seen her — I'd seen her reflection.

'We had them fitted right along the landing to make the place lighter,' he said. 'They're staggered, as you can see . . .'

When we did a quick test, we discovered that if Helen stood in the bedroom in front of her wardrobe with its door standing open, her reflection appeared on a succession of mirrors. There was a full-length mirror on the front of the wardrobe door and although she could never have been seen in her bedroom from the outside, the angle of that wardrobe mirror projected her image to one of the landing mirrors which in turn was picked up by another . . . and so the arrangement of the mirrors managed to provide that secret view — but only if the wardrobe door was standing open at a particular angle.

As we revealed this unexpected solution, Helen was walking around with her head in her hands, blushing and sighing and wondering how she could face the world, but her husband maintained he was proud that she could create such havoc, and said he would buy her a bottle of champagne at the races.

'Isn't there a horse called Mirror Mirror in the two-fifteen?' he then asked.

'I'll have to get some net curtains for that big window . . .' she was saying. 'And I must remember to keep my bedroom door closed when I'm changing. I knew those mirrors weren't a good idea, Geoffrey, it's like living in a house full of windows and no walls . . .'

'They do bring a bit of light on to that landing, darling, and it is very dark otherwise.'

'I don't know what people will think . . . those men . . . they must think I'm an exhibitionist or something . . .'

'I don't think so,' I said. 'It's only happened once or twice, since you became president I guess, and I don't think it will happen again. Happily, it seems to have solved my problem. Thanks for the coffee, I'll go and talk to Rudolph now. Your mum's going to miss all the excitement. I doubt there'll be any more unexpected callers — and she does make a super cup of coffee. And you'd better be off to York.'

'You won't broadcast this, will you, PC Rhea?' Helen's face was still a bright red.

'There's not a great deal of public interest in local accident prevention enquiries,' I smiled.

Unsure how to take my remark, Helen sneaked out of the back door without seeing Rudolph and I watched them drive away towards Lower Keld and the road to York. I hoped they had an enjoyable race meeting, for Helen did look stunning even with her clothes on. I would inform Sergeant Craddock of my discovery; I'd tell him there was no need to call in the Accident Prevention Department and went to join the others. I did wonder whether the reason for those accidents provided that wonderful defence of automatism — i.e. that the accident had happened due to an unexpected and unavoidable involuntary act, like sneezing, or being stung by a wasp. I doubted whether any court would regard the experience of admiring a lovely woman as an involuntary unavoidable action. But it had provided an interesting interlude in my daily work and, as I drove home, I thought I might even put a few shillings on Mirror Mirror in the 2.15 at York.

* * *

The incident with the mirrors caused me to reflect upon another series of comparable events, none of which could really be termed a road traffic accident even though all involved motor cars unwillingly running off the road. All these incidents happened in Elsinby — and all were associated with a reflection. Furthermore, they revealed the sheep-like propensity for motorists to follow one another without wondering why. A colleague once filled a charity event with motorists because, while performing traffic duty on a main road, he waved in a car which was displaying the requisite windscreen sticker. It turned down a drive to the event — which was charged at £1 per head — and before he could stop them, a dozen cars followed. There was mayhem in the small car park of the house at which the function was being held, but each had paid £1 before realising they weren't really supposed to be there. As one said, 'I thought it was a diversion of some kind, with a toll to pay.'

Elsinby is a pretty limestone village with a long main street. The pub, the Hopbind Inn, stands at one end of the wide street and in front of it there is a car park. The rest of that street comprises pretty houses and cottages, all set back from the road with gardens in front of them. As one enters Elsinby from the York direction, the pub is on the left, but flowing beside the street is Elsinby Beck, also on the left. This is a shallow stream, only five or six or inches deep, and it ripples over a bed of pebbles throughout its route along the village — and it flows right from one end of Elsinby to the other. Access to the houses at that side of the road is via a series of small bridges and the same applies to the Hopbind Inn, its bridge being rather wider than those of the houses.

Between the pub's bridge and the one next to it, however, is a long stretch of water, perhaps fifty yards, without a bridge — as the house at that point boasts a long garden. The stream, containing lots of grayling, therefore flows for that distance without any crossing place. From time to time, in the winter months or perhaps during some other rainy period, the stream rises but its gently sloping banks rise up to street level and are generally high enough to contain the extra depth. It's the kind of stream in which children can paddle safely in their wellies, with access from the road so smooth and easy. It is very rarely that Elsinby Beck overflows on to the street, but there have been times when it has been dangerously close to the top of its banks and there have been times, usually on a wet night, when it has been difficult to determine where the road ended, and the water began.

One June, shortly after my arrival as the village constable of Aidensfield, we experienced a dreadful summer with dense chilling fogs and repeated heavy and prolonged showers of rain. Elsinby Beck, along with other water courses on my patch, began to rise and there was concern that many rivers and streams would overflow their banks. In spite of the weather, however, determined holiday makers went about the business of enjoying themselves apparently undeterred by the unfriendly climate and many of them, particularly those from towns and cities, ventured into the countryside surrounding Aidensfield. Some came for day trips, others for longer periods. It was around that time that ordinary people found themselves with extra time for leisure, more money to spend and motor cars to carry them into rustic places. Some, however, were not really *au fait* with rural standards and conditions.

I realised that when I motored through Elsinby in my Mini-van on one of those damp, dismal and foggy June evenings because there was a car in Elsinby Beck. By the look of things, it had run off the road and was parked with the water midway up its wheels, but there was no one in attendance. It was not a local car — I would have recognised it — and a sticker in the rear window suggested it had come from a garage in Wakefield. My first inclination was that it was a stolen car which had been abandoned here, but when I radioed Force Control Room, they told me it had not been reported stolen, nor was it on any list of suspect vehicles. I could not check for the owner's name and address because it was after five o'clock and all the vehicle licensing departments would be closed. So I did the next best thing. I went into the pub to ask if anyone could enlighten me. The landlord, George Ward, noticed my arrival and left the bar to attend me. I noticed the pub was busy even though it was only 7.30.

'Early visit, Nick?' he asked. He was a round, happy individual and a most helpful person; he ran his enterprise with efficiency and humour, and there was never any public order problem for me to deal with at the Hopbind. That might have something to do with the fact that George was six foot six inches tall and as wide as the proverbial barn door.

'There's a car in the beck,' I said. 'Just up the road. I wondered if you knew who it might belong to.'

'Oh, yes. You see that chap with the white sweater, at the window table, with that redhead beside him? Having a snack? It's his. He's parked it there.'

'Parked it there?' I laughed.

'He thought it was a parking area at the side of the road. It was very dull, dark enough to put car lights on. The road surface was wet and shining with lots of reflection from car lights -just like the surface of the beck in fact. He didn't real-ise the shiny surface on his nearside was a stream, he thought it was part of the wet road. He drove straight in, down a bit of a slope, and got his feet wet climbing out. So he came here. He's decided to stay the night with his wife, and he'll get a garage to drag his car out tomorrow.'

'Not now?'

'There's no need, Nick, it's quite safe there, the water doesn't come up to the doors, so it hasn't got inside, and the beck won't rise overnight. He can dry his socks and shoes and trousers while he's here and so can she, and I get a pair of customers for bed and breakfast. No problems at all!'

'He's not hurt then?'

'No, not him. Do you want a word? You can go into my office if you like.'

'I'd better, just in case we get night patrols asking about it.'

George called the man over and I led him into George's cramped office; his name was Simon Newton and he lived in Wakefield. He was in his mid-fifties I reckoned, and he said he was a printer by trade, having a short holiday. I explained my interest and he shrugged his shoulders.

'There's no damage, Officer; me and the wife got wet feet but nothing else. It'll cost overtime to call a garage out tonight — I can't drive it out, there's no traction on those pebbles — so I thought it best to leave it till tomorrow. It's not taking water in, it's very shallow so it's quite safe. There's no problem is there?'

'George said you mistook the beck for the road surface?'

'I did. There's nothing to show where one stops and the other starts, is there? You locals know the water's there, but strangers like me don't. I'm surprised you've not had other folks driving into the beck like I did.'

'There might have been, without me knowing,' I smiled. 'Or perhaps it's just a fluke of circumstances tonight — a bit of fog, shining wet road surface, the need for lights even though it's not dark yet . . .'

'Could be,' he said. 'But I reckon you need something along the edge of the road, railings or a white line even, just to show daft motorists like me that I can't go any further.'

I debated in my mind as to whether or not this incident should be classified as a road accident and whether it was something I should record but decided against it. There was no damage or injury, no other vehicle was involved — all he'd done was park off-road in a damp place, so I decided not to take any further particulars. But, as I was leaving the office with Mr Newton, another man was coming into the pub, stamping his feet and dripping water everywhere. I was the first person he saw.

'Ah, the constabulary! Just the fellow. Do you realise that car park's flooded?' he said. 'Look at this, it's ruined my shoes . . .'

'What car park?' I asked, knowing the answer.

'Out there, I pulled in behind that other chap and bingo! I'm up to the hubcaps in water.'

'You've parked in the stream,' I said.

'Well, there's another car there, I thought it was a car park!'

'Sorry, but no,' I said. 'This is the other driver. He's been explaining to me how he mistook the beck for a car park.'

'Well, there's two of us there now, neatly parked I might add. So how can I get out?'

'If you drove in perhaps you can drive out?' I said.

'I can't, I've tried,' he said. 'The wheels just spin on the gravel or pebbles on the river-bed. It's like driving in snow. Is there a garage handy?'

'There's one in Aidensfield,' I said. 'It's shut now, but the owner lives next door. I'm going there now, I can take you.'

'Could you? I'm on my way home to Middlesbrough. It's been one of those days . . . are you sure it's not a car park? I pulled in because I thought I'd pop into that pub for a quick snack . . .'

His name was Colin Potter and when I pulled up in front of Bernie Scripps's garage with him aboard, Claude Jeremiah Greengrass happened to be parking his lorry outside the garage.

'Evening Claude,' I said.

'I'm parking here because the pub car park's full,' he grumbled. 'You're not going to shift me, are you?'

'No, I've come to see if Bernie will turn out; this gentleman needs to be towed out of Elsinby Beck.'

'Bernie will charge a fortune this time of night, I can do it for half his price,' he said without batting an eyelid. 'Right now. Immediately, if not sooner.'

And so the deal was done. I watched Mr Potter climb into Claude's battered old truck and did think the job would be done more swiftly than if Bernie had been involved — although I did not care to worry just how much Claude's half-price offer would be. The next day, I was off duty and because the children were at school and Mary had gone shopping with a friend, I decided to treat myself to a pub lunch at the Brewers' Arms in Aidensfield. When I walked into the bar, Claude hailed me.

'By gum, Constable, you did me a good turn last night. Five cars parked in that beck . . . they all thought it was a carpark and once they got in, they couldn't get out . . . all because that first chap went in. I pulled him out an' all, five cars at a quid apiece. A right good night's work. Let me buy you a drink!'

I accepted because a drink from Claude was indeed a rarity. Afterwards, I decided that I should refer the matter to Sergeant Craddock and so I submitted a written report, suggesting that a small white fence be erected alongside the stream to prevent further incidents of this kind. And so it was done. Since then, Elsinby Beck has not been used as a pub car park.

CHAPTER 4

One of the courtesy services provided by police officers was the supervision of unoccupied properties, usually when the owners were away on holiday or absent for some reason. Most police stations maintained an 'Unoccupied Property Register' and when an officer began his tour of duty, he would examine this book to see if any of the premises on his beat currently required attention. This was especially important during the night-time hours, but at all times the presence of a uniformed patrolling bobby in the vicinity was considered a good visible deterrent against local crooks, speculative burglars, housebreakers or travelling thieves.

Clearly, the police could not provide twenty-four-hour supervision, but if an unoccupied house was raided, it meant the crime would often be discovered by the police rather than await the return of the occupants — and early discovery increased the likelihood of the villains being caught. As more villains began to use motor vehicles to travel longer distances for their nefarious work, however, the chances of catching them were becoming increasingly remote. They could be miles away before the crime was discovered, and in many cases a professional burglar would have disposed of the ill-gotten goods at the earliest opportunity, thus ridding himself of any incriminating evidence.

In spite of this, we maintained our visits to unoccupied premises, which could include houses, shops, factories, warehouses, schools and any other kind of building, and there is no doubt our efforts did deter some criminals while providing some security in the minds of owners and occupiers.

Our service was free of charge too, which added to its popularity.

Among the regular users of my services in this respect were Mr and Mrs Galbreith, Bruce and Fiona, who lived at Thackerston Lodge. They were art dealers on a large scale and frequently kept valuable paintings and sculptures in their home. The valuables were always securely stored, but when the couple were going away on business, they would telephone and ask me to keep an eye on the house and outbuildings. Each time they rang, I assured them of my best attention and entered details in the 'Unoccupied Property Register' at Ashfordly Police Station. That meant my colleagues would also visit the house. During the absence of the Galbreiths, I would visit the house at least once during every tour of duty, and on a more regular basis if circumstances permitted. It is fair to say I never had any problems with their house; no one broke in and no one attempted to. And when the Galbreiths returned, one or other of them would ring to say 'thank you' while assuring me everything was in order.

On one occasion, however, I hadn't bargained for the presence of Claude Jeremiah Greengrass — not that he would break into anyone's house. But one evening in late March, Bruce Galbreith rang to say he and his wife would be going away for a couple of weeks beginning on 8 April. They would return on the evening of 21 April and the house would be empty during that time. They were going to Scandinavia on an art-buying trip, visiting dealers in Norway and Sweden, and Bruce provided me with their addresses, telephone numbers and personal contacts throughout the journey.

'There's just one thing, Mr Rhea,' he added, almost as an afterthought. 'I'm having some work done on the roof while we're away, repointing the ridges, replacing cracked tiles, having gutters cleaned, that sort of thing.'

'Thanks for telling me,' I responded. 'Who's doing the work?'

'Mr Greengrass has assured me he can do everything I require — I thought you ought to know he'll be around the premises from time to time. Or up on the roof to be precise. I have told my neighbours to expect him.'

'Thanks,' I said. 'He'll be no trouble — and if he's there, I doubt if any housebreaker will attempt to get in! And Claude himself is not a threat — we'll keep an eye on things for you.'

Thackerston Lodge is a splendid old house dating to the seventeenth century, but it has been frequently extended and modernised. This is evident when looking at the distinctive roof — or roofs. There are two distinct sections of roof, one running parallel with the other. It almost looks like two houses standing very close, side by side. At the eastern end of the house, a third roof runs at right angles which makes it appear as if a third cottage has been added. Inside, however, it is one large and glorious multi-roomed home.

That curious roof continues to excite interest even today. Lots of tall chimneys sprout from the complex of ridges, tiles and attic windows, but because there is a deep crevice between the two principal roofs, its guttering, lead flashings and drains require constant attention. If water is allowed to collect there, perhaps due to a drain being blocked with leaves, it would quickly find its way into the house.

It was essential that the area was well maintained, and I guessed that was one of Claude's tasks. During my first five or six visits, there was no sign of him then, one Friday morning, I spotted his old truck in the yard. It was a large yard, rather like the quadrangle of a country mansion and the truck was unattended. As I looked around the buildings, I found no sign of Claude, his side-kick David, or Alfred, his faithful dog. I made a rapid tour of the ground floor, checking doors and windows for signs of illegal entry and found none. There was nothing to suggest anyone was there or had been there. Slightly puzzled by the presence of the truck without any sign of its lord and master, I noted in my pocket book that the house had been secure during my inspection at 11.15 a.m., and then I left. I thought Claude must have popped into a neighbouring house for a quick coffee or to borrow something — that was quite usual — and I thought no more about the matter.

For me, that particular Friday was rather quiet with few pressing commitments and so, as I cruised through Thackerston around 4.30 that same afternoon, on my way home to book off duty, I decided I had time to pay a second visit to the Lodge. As I entered the yard, Claude's truck was still parked in exactly the same place and it was unattended as before. This time, though, I heard a shout from above and when I looked up, there was Claude high on the roof, shouting down to me and gesticulating wildly. He was standing on the wide stone ledge which surrounded the roof, forming a useful walkway to aid repairs and inspections. Many larger houses in this district had been constructed with those useful assets.

'You'll have to shout, Claude, I can't hear you!' I bellowed.

'I said what have you done with my ladder?' His voice sounded faint in its lofty position.

'Ladder? It's not here!' I opened my arms as if to emphasise its absence.

'I know it's not here, I can see it's not here, but it *was* here when I came up because I used it, and I've been up here all day trying to attract attention because I want to come down. And nobody's come close enough to see me! I've been wanting to come down for hours; I've missed my dinner and coffee breaks and things, and all I can say is it's a good job this spot has drains up here, I can tell you. Has it fallen then? Got blown over, or knocked over, or something?'

'Where was it?' was my next question.

'Right below where I'm standing,' he said.

'There's no sign of it now,' I shouted at him. 'Hang on, I'll have a look around. Somebody might have moved it . . . what's it like?'

'Like?' he bellowed. 'What do you mean, what's it like? It's like two long thin poles with a set of little steps up the middle . . .'

'Don't be daft, Claude, or I'll go away and leave you there. I mean, is it single length, or an extending ladder, or made of wood, or aluminium, or is it coloured, distinctive in any way? If I look in those sheds, I might find another ladder, not yours.'

'You're far too finicky, Constable, if you don't mind me saying so. Look, just find my ladder, or any ladder, and get me down, Alfred will want his tea. It wouldn't surprise me if he wants letting out an' all. Dogs need to go, like men.'

I had not seen a ladder either on the ground or standing against any of the walls during my earlier visit — I was sure about that. It was the sort of thing I would have noticed, but I told him I'd make a thorough search and then return.

'Don't go away!' I called.

'Go away? Where can I go?' he bellowed. 'You're enjoying this, aren't you . . . I bet you moved my ladder as a joke!'

'I didn't move it, but somebody else might have done,' I chuckled. 'Who have you been upsetting lately?'

'Upsetting? I don't go around upsetting folks, they go around upsetting me, like you're upsetting me right now. Look, just you go and find my ladder, then I can come down and we can all go home.'

I walked around the entire exterior of the house without finding any sign of Claude's ladder and then examined all the outbuildings. Most of them were securely locked, but several were not, chiefly because they contained nothing of value. The contents were cast furniture, logs and unwanted household items — not one of them produced a ladder of any description.

'No luck, Claude!' I called as I returned. 'Not a ladder in sight.'

'So how am I going to get down?' he demanded. 'And don't say jump, or I will, and I'll make sure I land on you — I need summat soft to break my fall.'

'I'll call the Fire Brigade,' I said. 'Ashfordly Fire Brigade is always looking for opportunities to practise their skills and it'll make a good story for the newspapers, far better than having a cat stuck up a tree.'

'Now you're getting ridiculous! Look, just pop into Fairclough's farm, he owes me a favour, He'll have a ladder, all farms have ladders. And make sure it's long enough to reach up here!'

Don Fairclough's farm was next door, but he was in Malton. His wife showed me an extending ladder which was propped against the side of a Dutch barn and she allowed me to borrow it to rescue Claude from his distress. Heavy and made of solid wood, it would be ideal for that purpose and so I shortened it, then lugged it the 300 yards or so to Thackerston Lodge. Panting with the effort, I extended it and with shouts of encouragement from Claude, leant it against a solid stone ridge. With a good deal of puffing and panting, he clambered aboard and began his descent.

'About time too! There's never a constable around when you want one so where's my ladder? Aren't you supposed to be keeping an eye on this house? Stopping folks nicking things?'

'What time did you go up to the roof?' I ignored his grumbles.

'Ten o'clockish. Why?'

'I came here about quarter past eleven,' I told him. 'I did a complete tour of the house, checking windows and things. Your truck was there, but I saw no sign of either you or a ladder. If there'd been a ladder up to the roof, I'd have seen it.'

'I was on the roof then, you'd not see me up there, not when I'm working in those middle bits. I put my ladder where you've put this one. And you say it's not lying around anywhere?'

'I've looked everywhere, Claude. You can check if you want, but I reckon it's gone.'

'That's typical, isn't it? Here's me doing an honest day's work and somebody comes along and nicks the tools of my trade. I could have been marooned up there for days, you realise that? Days!'

'Well, you weren't. It's a good job I happened to call back or you could have up there all night. Anyway, let's concentrate on the important issue. It seems there has been a crime, Claude, the theft of your ladder. So I shall need details before I can make a crime report, and then I can launch an investigation into the matter.'

'Launch an investigation? You mean ask a few blokes in the pub.'

'You'll want it back? Good ladders are expensive, and if you report it you can claim off your insurance.' I produced my pocket book and prepared to take notes.

'Insurance? What insurance?'

'You mean you're not insured for risks at work, like theft of your tools and so on?'

'I don't bother with insurance, Constable! Of course I'm not insured!'

'Well, do you wish to make a formal complaint of larceny?' I used the alternative word for theft which was then in vogue.

'Well, if it means I might get it back, then I suppose it's not a bad idea . . . it can't be far, can it?'

'You'd recognise it again? I mean, if we do trace it, could you say that it was your ladder? We need some means of positive identification.'

'It's made of wood; it's splattered with splodges of paint, all colours, it's a double extension ladder and it's got lettering down one side — Henry Armitage and Sons, Builders, in red paint.'

'Armitage from Elsinby?'

'Aye, he lent it to me.'

'So it's his ladder, is it?' I put to him.

'Aye, well,' and he blinked heavily. 'I suppose it is.'

'But you're the injured person?'

'Injured? I'm not injured . . .'

'It's a term we used in our reports, for victims of any kind. You're the victim, Claude, the ladder was stolen from you, even though it's not yours. You were the custodian?'

'You're using a lot of funny words.'

'But you had possession of that ladder? Legal possession, I mean?'

'Legal possession? Of course I had. I didn't nick it! It's not my ladder, I'll grant you that, but I was in lawful possession. Isn't that how you blokes phrase it? Lawful possession? That means I'd better report it, eh? Otherwise he'll be claiming the cost from me. And he might be insured, mightn't he?'

'I'm sure he is, Claude. So what's the value of this ladder?'

'Value? I've no idea.'

'Well, what would it cost to replace it?'

'Oh, well, thirty-five quid? Does that sound about right? It was top quality, none of your cheap stuff for Armitage.'

I made the necessary notes in my pocket book so that I could compile my crime report and then I said, 'Well, Claude, that's it. I'll circulate a description and I hope we get it back for you.'

'So what do I do in the meantime? About that roof?'

'Well, you'll have to borrow another ladder, Claude, or buy one of your own.'

'Criminals are worse than tax men, aren't they? Depriving the working man of his livelihood.'

'And you'd better take this one back to Mrs Fairclough.'

'Me?' he spluttered. 'I didn't bring it here!'

'It was brought for your convenience!' I snapped.

'Aye, you brought it, so you should take it back,' he grunted.

'We'll both take it back,' I said.

And so we did, with one of us at each end. Mrs Fairclough said she'd been happy to help Claude down from his predicament.

'So what happens now?' he asked when we returned to his truck. 'I'm still short of a ladder, and I need one to finish this job.'

'You could always ask Mrs Fairclough if you can borrow that one again, but I won't be around to help you carry it.'

'Aye, well, forget what I said earlier, I'm not on very good terms with old man Fairclough.'

'So that's why you didn't want to go back with the ladder! What have you done to upset him?'

'Nowt, it's him who's upset me . . . anyroad, that's water under the bridge, but next time I want to borrow a tractor, I won't ask him. Now, I think I know a chap I can ask about another ladder . . .'

'Why not buy your own, Claude?'

'What? And risk getting it pinched while I'm up it? Not likely! There's too many ladder thieves around here.'

'Well, I'll log this into our system and if Mr Armitage wants to claim off his insurance, his company will contact us. So that's it, Claude. Now, it's my teatime. I'm working overtime because of you.'

And so we parted.

Next morning, I drove into Ashfordly to deliver my crime report, and told Sergeant Craddock I would be asking around the villages, just in case anyone had seen the thief making off with Claude's ladder. It would be nice to record 'detected' against that crime. My first call was at Henry Armitage's builder's yard where I was greeted by one of his sons, John.

'Morning, Nick.' John was a lively thirty-five year old with a mop of ginger hair and a ruddy face. 'What can I do for you?'

'You lent Claude Jeremiah a ladder, I believe?'

'Yes, we did; well, I did, to be precise,' and I could see the puzzlement on his face.

'Has he been in touch with you about it?' I asked.

'No, that's the problem, he's never been in touch about it,' he laughed. 'Why, what's happened?'

'It's been stolen,' I said. 'Sometime yesterday, while he was on the roof at Thackerston Lodge.'

'You mean he was using it?' he chuckled. 'I had no idea . . . it wasn't stolen, Nick, I just recovered it. I lent it to him six or eight months ago; we've been trying to get it back ever since and he's been promising to return it, but he never has. So yesterday, I was driving past and saw it standing there without anybody in attendance. I thought he'd gone away and left it and thought it might get stolen, so I put it in my wagon. It wasn't stolen — I was just recovering my own ladder!'

'Is it here?'

'Sure.' He led me to a roofed shelter and there, hanging from supports on the wall, was the ladder which matched the description given by Claude.

'Crime solved?' he grinned.

'No crime!' I laughed, using the term I would now have to enter as the conclusion to this episode.

'Did you say Claude was using it at the time? I never saw him.'

'His truck was in the yard, well hidden from the road, and he was working on the roof, that middle part which is out of sight. He couldn't get down, and with the Galbreiths being away, he was marooned up there till I happened to see him. Half past four that would be. He was stuck on that roof all day.'

'That's brilliant!' he chuckled. 'It'll serve him right! I only lent it to him for a couple of days and he kept saying he'd fetch it back but never did. I like that tale, having him stuck on that roof and not being able to get down! It should be worth a few pints in the pub!'

And so the great Greengrass ladder mystery was solved, and I recorded the incident as 'no crime'. But the firm of Henry Armitage and Sons refused to lend it to Claude any more, and neither would anyone else loan him one, so Claude was compelled to purchase one of his own. It was second-hand, but it cost him £27.10s.0d.

'Now I am the injured person,' he grumbled next time I saw him. 'I get one ladder nicked and finish up paying for another! There's no justice . . .'

'Is it time to get your tools insured?' I suggested. 'Just in case a real thief comes along?'

'I might settle for painting my name on it,' he muttered. 'Just in case somebody borrows it and doesn't bring it back.'

* * *

In Claude's case, the ladder had not been stolen but the incident reminded me of other occasions where odd things had been illegally taken. In our county alone, during the 1960s, reported thefts included a military tank, a double-decker bus, a railway engine, several boats, a warehouse, and a whole range of garden furniture such as seats, statues, sheds, greenhouses, plants and even an ornamental bridge.

Cars, lorries and motor cycles were regular targets, although we felt it odd when someone stole a steamroller and a mobile crane. We chuckled when a shop owner purchased an Alsatian dog to guard his premises, because someone stole the dog and its supply of biscuits. Drinkers were fond of removing beer glasses from pubs, hotel guests were famously known for taking home towels and some would resort to nicking pictures from their hotel room walls, while coffee drinkers in cafés tended to take spoons as souvenirs. Students would regularly make off with trophies such as street signs, Belisha beacons, parking cones, orange lights from road works, village name-plates and even portable traffic lights. Sadly, however, we never did trace the person who stole six chimney pots from an hotel, or the thief who ran off with forty-eight brown shoes in various sizes, all for the male left foot.

We caught one thief who broke into chemists' shops on a regular basis to steal tins of Elastoplast sticking plaster — he kept them all at home, unopened — and there was another who unlawfully collected brass door knockers. When he was caught, his house contained over 800 knockers, but he used a door bell: I think he was afraid his knocker might be stolen. Other thefts included townie gardeners who removed stones from dry stone walls with which to fashion their suburban rockeries, those who took lorry loads of sand or pebbles from the beach and one who managed to strip all the turf from a large lawn.

In spite of this catalogue of misdemeanours, frequent or large-scale theft was not a serious problem in rural areas during the 1960s.

Most of us could leave our doors unlocked while we were out or leave our tools safely in the unlocked garden shed, or our valuables in the car. Rural life was vastly different from town life, however. A friend bought a house in south London and when the outgoing owners departed, they left behind a colossal lorry engine. It was in the garden and when my friend contacted the previous owners' estate agents, he was told the engine was no longer required as the previous owners had gone to live overseas. It had been abandoned, so he could keep it. He did not want an old, rusting, useless lorry engine, but it was now his problem. When he discussed it with one of his new neighbours, he was told, 'Put it on the street — somebody will steal it.' And so, with the aid of a few strong friends and some lifting gear, he put it outside his garden gate. Next morning, it had vanished, and no one had heard or saw that furtive operation.

Thefts are often very mysterious events because few are witnessed, and I was confronted with a particularly puzzling series. Like the vanishing lorry engine, no one saw or heard anything of the thief or thieves. Initially, there was no suggestion I was to have a crime wave on my patch, but it quickly became evident that incidents of villainy were soaring due to the activities of just one clever sneak thief.

The first intimation of this particularly uncomfortable crime wave came when Alec Harding hailed me as I drove through Aidensfield one Monday morning. At his signal, I eased my Mini-van to a halt outside the post office whereupon Oscar Blaketon materialised — I think he'd been working on his window display and upon noticing my arrival, decided he wanted a social chat.

By chance, he arrived at my side at the same time as Alec.

'How do, Sergeant.' Alec was a sturdy, jovial character in his seventies, a retired farmer who now ran a smallholding which produced a few vegetables alongside his clutch of hens, ducks and pigs. He kept the animals 'just to give me summat to get out of bed for, retired folks shouldn't sit around all day doing nowt'.

'I'm not the sergeant any more, Alec, I'm Mr Blaketon now. I've retired from coppering,' smiled Blaketon. 'If it's a police job, it's nothing to do with me. I'm sure the new regime at Ashfordly will cope with whatever problem you throw at them.'

''Morning, Alec, 'morning, Sergeant.' I reacted instinctively, I would find it difficult referring to Blaketon as Mr Blaketon and even more difficult calling him Oscar.

'I'll leave you,' Blaketon said. 'If Alec wants to talk business, I shouldn't be here.'

'Nay, lad, you can stay, it's not confidential; in fact you might be better hearing what I've got to say, as this affects the whole community, not just me. And with you being involved with Aidensfield, you might be able to help.'

'It all sounds very intriguing,' smiled Blaketon.

'So what's the problem, Alec?' I asked.

'Somebody's run off with my toilet seat,' he said in all seriousness.

'Most inconvenient,' I agreed.

'Irritating, I'd say,' Alec scowled.

'Toilet seat?' I could see the beginnings of a smile on Blaketon's face. 'Why would anybody steal a toilet seat?'

'To sit on?' I said.

'Folks'll pinch owt these days,' said Alec. 'My pal's had three garden gnomes nicked from his garden in York, and they'd have had his little windmill if it hadn't been concreted in. Anyroad, I thought I'd better mention this business, you might come across it in your travels. Not that I want to make a fuss, but I thought you should know.'

'If thieves are about, we should know,' I agreed. 'So what's it look like?'

'Polished wood, ash mebbe, very smooth and well-worn, nicely shaped, very comfortable an' all. You could sit there all day with a good book. I've a copy of *Encyclopaedia Britannica* in there . . . very informative, it is.'

'Did it have a lid?' I asked. 'The seat, I mean, not the encyclopaedia.'

'No, no lid,' said Alec. 'Open and ready for action, it was.'

'Value?' was my next question.

'How can you put a value on a toilet seat, Nick?' he asked. 'It'll be an antique I reckon, and the wood alone will be worth a few bob, very well crafted it is; then if we don't track it down I've got to find a new 'un, and I'd say new seats cost quite a bit these days . . . I wonder if my insurance covers it?'

'Shall we say three pounds?' I put to him. 'I need a value for my crime report.'

Blaketon stood and listened to this interchange with a look of bemusement on his face.

'Well, Nick,' he said. 'I can see this is going to keep you busy for the next few months, house-to-house enquiries, examining all toilet seats in Aidensfield to see if they match the stolen one, trying to catch the thief red-handed, keeping observations in likely places.'

'If it's a crime,' I said, 'it will receive every consideration!'

'This will be a testing time for Sergeant Craddock too. His first really serious outbreak of crime, I would imagine,' grinned Blaketon.

Now that he was no longer a member of the Force, I could see Oscar Blaketon was enjoying this — and I knew he would love to see Sergeant Craddock's face when I submitted this report. But I ignored his taunts — I had no intention of sitting all night in a toilet to maintain observations just in case a thief came along.

'So where did it go from?' I asked.

'That toilet down my smallholding,' said Alec. 'My outside loo. It's a WC, by the way, with a light in as well, all mod. cons. Very cosy if I might say so. I used it a lot when I was working outside. I could sit in there and read for hours. And it meant I didn't have to take my wellies off whenever I got taken short. The missus doesn't like me traipsing into the house with mucky feet.'

Most of the properties in Aidensfield had outside toilets at that time, although many of the houses were being updated with modern bathrooms. There was still a feeling among the older people, however, that it was rather unseemly to have a toilet indoors — the older people had been brought up to use earth closets which were necessarily as far away from the house as they could be.

In fact, a considerable number of people continued with their outdoor facilities in spite of having modern bathrooms fitted. But it seemed Alec had both.

'It reminds me of that old joke,' beamed Blaketon, who was clearly in a mischievous mood. 'When somebody nicked the toilet seat from a police station a police spokesman said, "We are making enquiries, but at the moment we've got nothing to go on".'

'Do you have an outside toilet, Mr Blaketon?' I put to him as a means of countering his banter.

'Yes, at the bottom of my garden. Why?'

'I just wondered if your seat was where it should be?'

'Well, I haven't checked for a while, we don't use it that much . . . this house has all mod cons, you know.'

'Just a thought,' I smiled.

'Well, if you want, I'll go and check. You'd better come with me, just in case my nessie has become the scene of a crime.'

And so both Alec and I followed him through the post office and into the garden at the rear. It was a long garden with a brick-built toilet at the distant end and, like all these gardens, it led into a back lane which served all the properties. And when he opened the toilet door, the seat was missing.

'Well, I'll be damned!' he said. 'It's gone!'

'And now you've nothing to go on,' I smiled.

'Why would anybody pinch my toilet seat?' he frowned.

'To sit on?' I smiled.

'This is no joke, Nick.'

'I wonder how Sergeant Craddock will respond to this one, Mr Blaketon?' I smiled now. 'I'm sure he'll do everything within his power to trace the culprit, so I shall need a statement from you after I've taken one from Alec. Shall I get the Scenes of Crime lads to come and examine the area for footprints and so on?'

'Look, I don't think I need to make an official report of this, do I?' Blaketon was blushing now. 'I mean, if I am seen to be the victim of a crime within such a short time of retiring, and especially a crime of this sort, that new sergeant of yours is going to make whoopee at my discomfort . . .'

'I thought it was unlawful to conceal a crime, Mr Blaketon?' I liked his choice of words but did not comment upon them.

'We do not know with certainty that there has been a crime,' he countered. 'There may be some other explanation.'

'I've always understood that where a series of crimes was committed, it was essential to examine each report in detail so that links might be established and evidence found which might lead to the arrest of the person or persons responsible.'

'As I said,' he muttered, 'there is no proof that my loss is a crime. I need to make my own enquiries. After all, I had no idea of this until now.'

'Well mine's a crime,' said Alec. 'It was there on Friday night and it's gone this morning. Unscrewed and swiped.'

'Your wife hasn't removed it for cleaning, has she?' I asked.

'No, I asked her. It wasn't on her cleaning list and she hasn't taken it. Nobody's been to my smallholding over the weekend 'cos we've been there all the time, and I haven't removed it. So mine's been nicked. There's no doubt about it.'

As we stood gazing at Blaketon's seatless toilet, I said, 'Well, it seems to me that we have a habitual toilet-seat stealer. The theft of one seat might be the work of somebody who's cracked his own seat and can't afford to buy a replacement, but two seats indicates a series of serious crimes. I shall commence enquiries, and I hope you gentlemen will do likewise — what we need is a common factor—'

'They're both toilet seats,' grunted Blaketon. 'There's your common factor.'

'Yours was a wooden one, was it?' I asked. 'So when did it disappear?'

'Yes, it was wood, nicely shaped like Alec's, beech I would guess, although I couldn't be sure, and I've no idea when it was last here. I've not been in here since a week last Friday.'

'Maybe it disappeared that following weekend, Sergeant?' I still found myself calling him Sergeant. 'Maybe there's a phantom toilet-seat nicker at large in Aidensfield, operating only at weekends?'

'That's something for you to sort out,' he grinned.

'So I shall report yours as a crime?' I said.

'If you must,' he consented, somewhat grudgingly.

And so I took sufficient details for my crime reports, had a quick look at each of the scenes of crime, and later telephoned Sergeant Craddock with the news. After I had explained the circumstances of each crime, Craddock said, 'Two crimes to add to your annual statistics, PC Rhea—' I could hear the humour in his voice — 'and one of them with ex-Sergeant Blaketon as the victim. How interesting. Someone with a grudge against him, do you think?'

'I doubt it.' I didn't regard this as a vengeance type of crime. 'He wasn't the only victim and I can't see anyone wishing to harm Alec Harding, or to cause him any kind of misery.'

'Well, you never know, do you? I am sure some would wish Blaketon a little private discomfort, but I must not make fun of a victim of crime. You will commence enquiries?'

'Immediately, Sergeant,' I asserted.

'I don't want this to develop into an epidemic of looted loo seats, PC Rhea. Put yourself about, show the uniform at the likely scenes of future crimes, deter the thief from repeating his felonies and catch him red-handed if you can. Or her.'

As I left to return to my beat, I wondered if both Blaketon and Alec had been victims of some kind of practical joke, perhaps in revenge for something they'd said or done in the past. I spent time talking to both in an effort to identify a common factor but produced nothing, nor did I find anyone who'd seen characters acting suspiciously in the vicinity of the victimized nessies. Then another seat vanished.

Miss Felicity Farrell, a spinster of the parish aged about sixty-five, delicately informed me that someone had stolen the seat of her outdoor toilet. During the weekend, it had vanished from the bottom of her garden. It was made of wood.

Then Aaron Newberry reported one of his missing — he had two loos side by side behind his large house, and the wooden seat from one of them had vanished — but this time, he could pin the time down to between 6 p.m. on the Saturday and 9 a.m. on the Sunday. He had been into his toilet block because he kept his gardening tools there.

I began to think the thefts were the work of someone coming home from the pub after having supped a little too much; one common factor was that each was taken from an outside toilet at the distant end of the domestic garden, and each was accessible by a back lane. The chances of anyone being seen at night in such a place was quite remote. Apart from that, there were plenty of places to hide, such as lots of outside toilets. None of the losers had heard any voices or sounds of a motor vehicle in their back lanes at night which made me think the thief was on foot. A further thought was that the perpetrator was probably a loner. Man or woman? Adult or child? Local person or travelling thief? I had no idea.

I decided to visit the pub in uniform each time I was working a late shift, chiefly to see if any of my local loners and shifty types were drinking; I would bid them all a cheery goodnight but would not go to bed. I would conceal myself in the shadows of those lanes to undertake a spot of loo-watching as they returned home. The snag was there were several miles of winding lanes around the village, any one of which they might use, but I had to do something positive. My pub visits convinced me that the Saturday night regulars were there, and I quietly took note of them all, bearing in mind my growing knowledge and suspicions.

While I was doing this, two more outdoor loo seats vanished, one from the village school's ancient toilets and another from the rear of Ash House, home of a Mr and Mrs Williamson. There may have been others which had not been reported to me. But by this stage, however, I felt I was closing in on a suspect because I'd noticed the presence of a youth called Gary Drummond.

Gary was well known around Aidensfield because most people felt sorry for him. His father had run off with a bus conductress when Gary was only three years old, but already it was clear by then that Gary was rather mentally under-developed. His mother, Amy, had brought him up with as much love and care as she could muster but Gary would never be anything more than a rather dim-witted fellow. He was not certifiable, however, and now, aged eighteen, he could work at menial tasks. At school, he had tried very hard to join things like the football and cricket teams, the annual Christmas pantomime and other activities, but no one would select him for their team games. He spent a lot of time alone, just watching the others. Now that he was eighteen, he ventured into the Brewers' Arms but inevitably drank alone unless some of the others plied him with drink, hoping for some kind of fun with the poor lad. But George Ward, the licensee, kept an eye on things — he protected Gary against the wiles of those who would tease or take advantage of him. I felt he was a good candidate for my suspicions but had no idea why he would do such a thing. There were various ways I could tackle the problem — I could wait until I could follow him in the darkness one night, hoping to catch him in the act of stealing, or I could visit his home and ask his mother if I might look into his bedroom.

As things worked out, I found myself undertaking the former simply because I'd been performing a late patrol in Ashfordly, and on my way home spotted Gary leaving the Brewers' Arms. I slid the van into a convenient side road, switched off the lights and engine, and set about following Gary on foot. I armed myself with a very powerful torch. Sure enough, he took a route along one of the back lanes and the reflected light of the houses was sufficient for me to keep him within my sights. He'd had a few drinks — I could see that by the haphazard way he walked — and he was singing very quietly to himself as he made his way home. I didn't think his music could be heard by anyone indoors. After moving along the lane, I saw him open a rear garden gate and disappear. I slid into a convenient shadow and waited. After about ten minutes, Gary emerged — and in the reflected glow I could see he was carrying a toilet seat — its lighter shade was easy to recognise. He must have had a spanner to loosen the nuts, and a torch to light his work, but now he'd put his arm through it and he wore it like a huge bracelet, albeit around his shoulder.

I could have arrested him there and then but decided to follow him all the way home because I wanted to know where he took the seats and what he was doing with them. He ceased his singing on that final part of his journey and I saw him let himself into the house, still with the seat on his arm. It was time to act. I went to the door, rang the bell and Mrs Drummond, still in her day clothes, answered. Now in her fifties, she looked grey and tired.

'Oh, Mr Rhea! Good heavens! At this time of night! What is it?'

'Is Gary in?' I asked.

'Oh, dear, is something the matter?'

'I'd like to talk to him,' I told her gently. 'You'd better come with me.'

'He's been out for a drink, with his friends, he does that on a Saturday. He'll be in his room. I wait up for him, to make sure he comes home, and he always goes straight upstairs . . .'

She led me up the stairs and I saw the light peeping from under his door, then Mrs Drummond said, 'Gary, PC Rhea wants a word with you. I hope you've not been doing wrong.'

Sheepishly, Gary opened his door just a fraction and peered out, 'Hello, Mr Rhea.'

'Hello, Gary,' I smiled at him. 'Can I come in?'

'What do you want?'

'I think you know what I want, Gary. Come along, let us in, me and your mum.'

After pausing for a long moment, Gary opened his door wide and I went in, followed by Mrs Drummond. The first thing I saw was an array of toilet seats fixed to his bedroom walls, each with a newspaper photograph in the centre, and each with a splodge of black paint over the photo. The seats were all serving as frames for the photographs, except his latest acquisition, which was still on his bed.

'What is it, Mr Rhea?' Mrs Drummond was worried and puzzled, clearly having no idea Gary had been stealing these odd objects.

'He's not had permission to take these seats, have you, Gary?'

'He told me the people gave them to him! His friends at the pub, he said.'

'No, he's been stealing them, Mrs Drummond, sneaking into outdoor toilets on his way home from the pub.'

'Oh, Gary how could you!' She began to weep softly, and I felt sorry for her, but I had a job to do.

'Why, Gary?' I asked. 'Why take these seats?'

I looked closer at the newspaper photographs which were enclosed in these distinctive frames — one was the Aidensfield football team, another was the cricket team, and I saw the Brewers' Arms darts team, the snooker team and other events, including a golf team in which the Brewers'

74

Arms had competed against a team from the Hopbind Inn at Elsinby. And all were covered with a splash of black paint.

'They never let me join,' he said quietly. 'I'm no good, they say, for the cricket and whatever, so I framed them all, like this, and threw muck at them . . .'

'Oh, Gary,' Mrs Drummond put her arms around his shoulders. 'What am I going to do with you?'

'I'll have to take him with me, Mrs Drummond; you'd better come too, to Ashfordly Police Station.'

With help from Gary and Mrs Drummond, I loaded the toilet seats into my Mini-van; Mrs Drummond sat in the front passenger seat and Gary was in the rear, looking after his seats. I radioed ahead — being a Saturday night, Sergeant Craddock was still on duty, and he took my call.

'You'll be relieved at my news, Sergeant. I've caught the toilet-seat thief, I'm on mv way to Ashfordly with him right now. And I have twelve toilet seats as evidence, all recovered intact.'

Later, the seats were returned to the losers (after a formal identification parade of the seats) and Gary was put on probation, with professional help being made available for him. Funnily enough, when the story circulated in the village, the cricket team seconds invited him to play at No. 11.

He scored two runs and he never stole any more toilet seats.

CHAPTER 5

When Johnny Holidaymaker decides to drive his car away for the weekend or for a longer break, it is not unknown for him to forget to top up the radiator with water, check the oil, blow up the spare tyre, or even fill the tank with sufficient fuel to reach his destination. As a consequence, the routes to our tourist-filled destinations are frequently littered with stranded day-trippers, some of whom stand forlornly by cars which steam and smoke like erupting volcanoes, while others make pleas for receptacles capable of holding a drop of petrol, so they can take it to the nearest oasis, fill it up and so get back on the road to the heaven for which they yearn. It's amazing how far some motorists think they can travel on an empty tank.

Advance planning or adequate preparation seems to be a skill unknown to many and it is then that the emergency services, like the AA or RAC, have to deal with the problem. If the motor car makes a sudden and involuntary decision to stop, of course, then the police may be called to deal with the resultant accident, traffic jam or road blockage. It is not surprising, therefore, that many police officers feel that such thoughtlessness among motorists should be penalised, perhaps by making them pay for the cost of the disruption for which they are so often responsible.

While I was engaged in policing the North York Moors during the 1960s, traffic was considerably less than the period in which these notes are being written (AD 2000) but even at that time, holiday motorists seemed to have a wonderful capacity for doing stupid things, often to the consternation and disruption of those around them.

A regular lapse was — and still is — for a driver to set sail for his holiday destination without a map and, as the geographical knowledge of many drivers seems to be nil, it is not surprising they get lost. For example, I was patrolling Aidensfield one morning around eight o'clock when a small car drew to a halt beside me. It contained two people, a middle-aged man and his wife and when they spoke, I realised they had come from Scotland.

'Excuse me,' said the gentleman, 'but could you tell me the way to Derby?'

Gently, I explained that Derby was about 155 miles to the south, suggesting he make his way to York and then ask directions to the Al, the Great North Road. 'If you get to London,' I joked, 'turn back, you'll be on the wrong road again.'

'Is London before or after I get to Derby?' he asked.

'After, if luck is on your side,' I returned.

I discovered the couple were making their way from Perth to Derby and had somehow become hopelessly lost in the middle of the North York Moors, miles away from their direct route. How on earth they had found their way to Aidensfield during that journey remains a mystery.

In another instance, our Force Control Room received a call from a gentleman living in Edinburgh. After apologising for troubling us with his domestic arrangements, he said his mother was driving down from Edinburgh to Hemel Hempstead the following day and he was advising the control room of every police headquarters *en route,* providing them with her name and the registration number of her car.

When our control room operator asked why we should wish to know this, the man said, 'Well, my mother can't make right-hand turns, so I have produced a route for her which does not have any — it's only got left-hand turns, straight aheads and roundabouts.'

We assured him we would keep an eye open for her. She did get lost, as one might have expected, and we found her cruising around Thirsk in a state of some bewilderment. We returned her to the Al with suitable advice — i.e., 'Don't turn left or right until you see the signs for St Albans and then Hemel Hempstead — it's only two hundred and fifty miles away'. Her son rang later to thank us for our attention, adding that his mother's journey had taken five days longer than anticipated during which time she'd managed to visit Durham, Thirsk, Pontefract, Retford, Nottingham, Loughborough, Coventry and Bicester. By the time she arrived, she'd forgotten why she'd set off in the first place.

Most police officers can tell tales of people becoming hopelessly lost, either because they did not have a map with them, or because they did not possess an elementary knowledge of map reading. One source of constant amazement is how many people manage to enter a dual carriageway the wrong way in the face of oncoming traffic. One hears tales of drivers spending hours on ring roads without knowing how to divert from these eternal roundabouts, but I like the story of the American tourist who, in the 1960s, had hired a car, only to find himself lost in the centre of ancient York. He toured the city centre for hours because he could not find a way out of the traffic system, then with great relief, he spotted a policeman.

'Say, Officer,' he sighed. 'How do I get outa this goddam museum?'

One of the most irritating motorized problems is the caravan. In rural areas, they clog up the roads, hinder moving traffic and, due to the inefficiency of some drivers, frequently cause mayhem along the so-called caravan routes. I know, because I live on such a route. And, of course, they occupy twice as much road space as a single motor car. Over the years, their numbers have proliferated to such an extent that in some places, on Friday evenings in summer, there is a constant procession of lumbering white mobile homes, like a circus on the move, or an army of white monsters determined to desecrate the landscape. On one local outing, I found myself coming up behind a line of seven caravan units, all moving sedately along a narrow country lane so tightly one behind the other that nothing could overtake them. People on business, doctors, vets, the emergency services, people returning from work and many others were compelled to follow this crocodile of unforgiving road-blockers who, after all, were merely going on holiday. They left no gaps which would allow a car to overtake the procession one by one, and not one of them offered to ease into the side of the road to permit the build-up of traffic to pass. That kind of frustration is now of increasing concern to rural dwellers who, it should not be forgotten, actually live and work in the countryside all year round, not just at weekends. Farm workers on tractors or those towing agricultural machinery will inevitably pull into the first available space to allow the build-up of traffic to overtake them, but selfish town-bred caravanners rarely do so. They seem determined to make other motorists proceed at their pace.

They do this even when *not* towing their monstrous mobile mansions — they can be identified by the tow bars at the rear. Rural dwellers often ask — why are caravanners so obdurate? And why are they so unskilled in their driving and towing techniques? And why do they rejoice in being such a confounded nuisance to other road users? And even when *not* towing their mobile homes, why do so many of them drive slowly down the middle of the road and never allow anyone to overtake?

Most rural police officers can tell horror stories of caravanners who have come to grief through bad driving, stupidity, ignorance of matters like weight distribution or the required towing strength of their cars, a total inability to reverse a caravan or, quite simply, a lack of essential basic skills. On one occasion, after I had retired from the police, I witnessed a caravan driver who drove his unit towards a road block. He had already passed several advance signs which announced the closure and provided a diversionary route, but he halted at the barrier which bore a sign saying 'Road Closed'. The barrier extended completely across the highway and comprised a large wooden bar, painted red. At that stage, he proceeded to remove the barrier, dragging the huge bar to the side of the road, and then, unbelievably, he drove his caravan unit through. He found himself among a galaxy of road repair vehicles and digging machines because the road was being dug up to replace an old water main. The entire village was temporarily closed to through-traffic and, when he arrived, there was absolutely no way through. Having found himself at a point where he could go no further, our genius decided he should turn around and leave.

The sight of him trying to reverse and turn around his caravan unit among a mass of diggers, concrete mixers, mobile cranes, dumper trucks, piles of earth and huge holes in the road was a wonder to behold. He caused absolute mayhem, held up work, and created more than a few rising tempers before the workmen came to his aid with a driver more skilled than he — matters had reached a point where all the contractors wanted was for this clown to disappear from their lives. It took almost an hour to extricate him from those road works. But why did he decide to drive through a 'Road Closed' sign? Was it because he knew he was incapable of reversing his unit? Even now, caravanners drive along roads bearing signs which say, 'Not suitable for caravans'.

Happily, shortly before compiling these notes, a licence and driver-testing system was introduced for those who wish to tow caravans. Prior to that, it was utterly illogical that an inexperienced person could hitch one of those huge monstrosities to the rear of his car and take it on the busy highway without any form of training, testing or licensing.

One of the enduring tales of caravanners is the one about the unit which pulled into a garage forecourt to fill up with petrol. The driver's mother-in-law was travelling in the van because there was no room in the car (an illegal act, by the way) but when the unit halted at the garage, she jumped out to pop to the toilet — and no one noticed. While she was thus engaged, her son-in-law filled up and paid his bill, then drove away without her. Marooned at the garage, she had no idea where their intended camping site was to be found, except it was somewhere on the coast near Scarborough.

She did not know the registration number of the car and had no contact name or telephone number with her. All she could do was sit and wait. In time, of course, the son-in-law reached his destination about an hour later and only then discovered her absence. It took another hour or more for him to return to collect her. I was told that tale by a garage owner — but it is told so frequently that one must wonder whether it is one of those wonderful urban legends.

Most police officers can provide entertaining tales of silly caravanners, but it was the actions of a little man called Elton Duff-Jones who, among the many lunatic caravanners that I encountered, made the biggest impression. Elton, an assembly line worker by profession, lived in a terraced house somewhere near the centre of Birmingham. His household included his wife, two teenage children, a Labrador called Ben and a spaniel called Charlie. Elton and his family liked nothing better than to venture into the countryside at weekends and for longer holidays — always with the caravan. One summer, he decided to spend a week caravanning in the lowlands of Scotland, followed by a second week doing likewise in *the* North York Moors. Had the inhabitants of Elton's destinations had prior knowledge of his intended presence, I'm sure they would have volunteered to fly to the moon, the South Pole or some other place as far as possible from Elton's caravan unit.

I have no idea what happened when he arrived in Scotland, but I shall never forget his arrival on the edge of the North York Moors. With his caravan behind his car, he drove from Scotland via the accepted routes to the North Riding of Yorkshire, using main roads from the Scottish borders.

He then followed the A1 to a point south of Scotch Corner. There he sought the junction which took him to Thirsk, and from Thirsk he looked for the A170 which he knew would take him through Ryedale to Pickering, a quiet market town on the southern slopes of the moors. Elton was heading for a caravan site close to the outskirts and his map clearly identified the route. It also showed, with a system of arrow-head markings, that there were several very steep hills along the way but Elton either ignored or didn't understand those indicators on his map. After all, he had coped with the hills of Birmingham!

Leaving Thirsk *en route* for Pickering on that hot summer Saturday afternoon, Elton and his entourage arrived at the foot of Sutton Bank. There were advance warning signs, including some which announced the length of the hill (one mile), and the fact that it rose in three successive gradients — 1-in-4 (25 per cent), 1-in-5 (20 per cent) and finally another climb of 1-in-4 (25 per cent).

Perhaps, at this stage, I should mention that Elton's car was a Morris 1000 Traveller, a small type of estate car with a wooden frame around the rear window section. Travellers were very popular in the 1960s. They were delightful small vehicles, ideal for people with dogs and small families — but Elton was towing a caravan. I would have thought that a car with such a small engine was not very suited for towing a loaded trailer of any kind, let alone a caravan. But, happily, I am not a caravanner, nor do I have any desire to become one! However, Elton's wife was not the smallest of ladies either, and neither were his children — Derek, aged fifteen, and Deborah, aged thirteen.

They were built in a similar style to their mother; she filled the front passenger seat and they filled the rear seat along with some of their more precious belongings. In the back of the Traveller were the dogs, the Labrador and the spaniel, separated from the passengers by a wire mesh partition.

Because the family was packed so tightly into the little vehicle, their holiday luggage — enough for two adults and two teenagers — was carried in the caravan, along with enough tinned food and drinks to sustain them during their two-week holiday. No one in their right mind would attempt to climb Sutton Bank with such a loaded unit but Elton was a caravanner of considerable experience and no hill had previously caused him concern. Like a knight going into battle, Elton rammed his foot on the accelerator, aimed his bonnet at the first gradient and, I suspect, said a little prayer. Somewhat amazingly, he surmounted the first gradient perhaps aided by the speed he had generated, but the second climb followed almost immediately, and it was there that the gallant little Traveller refused to go any further. It came to a shuddering halt. Elton and his family were thus marooned on the steep slope.

At that time, there lived nearby a hillside farmer who made a useful income by using his tractor to rescue caravanners in the Elton mould who failed to ascend Sutton Bank. There were lots of them in the summer months and at the sight or sound of distress, he would appear to offer his services — at a cost. Most were more than willing to pay his fees. The nearest garage with a breakdown truck was three miles away, so the farmer performed a useful service to stranded caravanners — but on that particular afternoon he had gone to Thirsk Races.

Elton, in those awful first moments, had no idea of that additional factor — it meant, of course, that there was no one immediately available to assist him. However, because he had come to rest on the nearside of the road, the other traffic was able to pass him, both on the ascent and descent. Unfortunately, he very quickly realised that his brakes were not holding him. The entire unit was beginning to move backwards down the hill and so he decided he should engage reverse gear and endeavour to guide his recalcitrant unit into a layby which was only a matter of yards behind him. Sadly, Elton's skills did not really encompass the reversing of a loaded caravan, and most certainly his expertise did not meet the demands of guiding one backwards down a gradient of 1–in-5 with traffic passing all the time, dodgy brakes and a car full of dogs, kids and a substantial wife.

Because the unit was beginning to gather speed as it threatened to escape backwards down the hill, he could not unload anyone or anything and so he only attempted to execute that reverse manoeuvre into the layby. Like the caravanner I mentioned earlier, he made a complete debacle of the operation. All other motorists going up and down the hill, now halted to observe this comedy of errors — and to keep a safe distance from the impending disaster but Elton could not reverse his caravan into the desired refuge; it went everywhere except where he wanted and finally he succeeded in backing it into the rock face which formed one side of the hill. The caravan came to rest at an acute angle across the road with the little Traveller still attached — and by now, of course, the entire unit was blocking both carriageways.

On the credit side, it meant the immediate emergency was over because the downward run of the unit had been halted, but it also meant that Sutton Bank, one of the busiest roads for holiday traffic at that time of year, was solidly blocked. The caravan could not run away due to the mountain of rock which retained it, so the family and the dogs climbed out with some relief. After some debate with other motorists, Elton decided he must have the services of a heavy-duty breakdown vehicle, something strong enough to tow the whole lot to the summit. He sent his son, Derek, to the hilltop to find a telephone kiosk.

Happily, there was one which was widely used by people in a similar plight, but because Elton had forgotten to give Derek some money, Derek exercised his initiative and dialled 999. The call was eventually dealt with by our Force Control Room; I happened to be patrolling in the vicinity in my Mini-van and was despatched to the scene to try and sort out the increasing traffic chaos. A diversion was suggested as we attempted to clear the blockage. Upon arrival, I drove down the hill, on the wrong side of the road which, of course, bore no oncoming traffic, and made a rapid assessment of the situation.

If I asked all the down-facing marooned drivers to turn around within the limited space of the highway and head back the way they had come, we could clear some of the backlog — I could then block the top of the bank with my parked van, put out my portable *POLICE DIVERSION* sign and arrows to prevent others from descending, and then await the arrival of a breakdown truck. After that, I'd return to wait with Elton and his caravan while redirecting ascending vehicles.

It is not necessary to record details of the rescue operation, save to say that the breakdown driver advised the unloading of both the Traveller and caravan so that both could be drawn safely from their resting place and realigned. Elton had then to be persuaded to drive his Traveller to the hilltop while allowing the breakdown truck to cope with the caravan, starting in the middle of such a steep hill not being the easiest of operations. Once at the top with his car, Elton and family would then have to walk up and down to retrieve their luggage, piece by piece.

The whole operation took more than two and a half hours; the only person who made a few pounds from the rescue was the breakdown vehicle driver. For all the trouble he had caused, it cost Elton nothing more, even though hundreds of motorists had been inconvenienced and delayed through his doltish behaviour. But that's all part of constabulary duties — we spend a lot of time dealing with problems caused by other people. And within an hour of concluding that incident, I was called to another caravan which had overturned on a sharp corner . . .

I wonder why rural dwellers dislike or mock these dreadful seasonal invaders?

* * *

In legal terminology, caravans and other trailers are not motor vehicles but there is a bewildering range of contraptions on our roads which do fit that category. Motor bikes, scooters, cars, vans, lorries, buses, road rollers, mobile cranes, heavy locomotives, heavy motor cars, light locomotives, invalid carriages, tractors, and all sorts of other things can be accommodated within the all-embracing term of 'motor vehicle'.

Even steam rollers or electrically propelled vehicles fit the description because the type of mechanical power includes that which comes from any source except manpower. A pedal cycle or a pram, therefore, is not a motor vehicle.

When I was the village constable of Aidensfield, the definition of a motor vehicle was 'a mechanically propelled vehicle intended or adapted for use on roads' which meant that if someone built a mechanically propelled vehicle specifically for use on a road, then it would be classified as a motor vehicle even if it looked abnormal. If it was a motor vehicle, then it required registration plates, tax, insurance, lights, brakes and all the other requirements of the Motor Vehicle (Construction and Use) Regulations before it could be legally used on a road.

From time to time, we had to contend with inventive wizards who fitted little motor engines to roller skates and chugged along the roads upon them — but if those skates had been adapted for use on a road, then they were motor vehicles! I suppose a pair of such skates would be two motor vehicles, requiring double tax, insurance and so forth!

It followed that the word 'adapted' caused some discussion — could a person 'adapt' something simply by using it? Or does the word 'adapt' suggest some physical alteration, change or improvement? From time to time, diligent constables would halt building-site dumper trucks when they were being driven along a road, perhaps to check a driving licence or to accuse the driver of speeding, but most courts decided these were not 'motor vehicles' because they were not constructed or adapted for use on a road — they were constructed or adapted for use on building sites.

Similarly, when the go-kart craze began in the 1960s, some people took them on the roads but a case *(Burns* v. *Currell,* 1963) decided a particular go-kart was not a motor vehicle because there was no evidence of its regular use upon the road. The occasional trip did not elevate it to the status of a motor vehicle. So what about a hovercraft? The law said this was a motor vehicle even though it hovered above the road surface on a cushion of air.

As a village constable in a very rural area, one never felt that such very fine distinctions would cause a problem, but I had not bargained for the inventiveness of a man called Clarence Gibbons. Clarence, who was married to Emily, was in his fifties when I arrived in the village, and the couple had no children. Clarence was a tall, gangly and rather untidy individual whose light-brown hair was always in need of a trim, whose face was eternally bewhiskered with a few days' growth and whose clothing looked as if it had been slept in. He tended to wear loose-fitting, or even baggy, brown tweed suits, dark-green shirts and woollen ties and he moved around Aidensfield with an everlasting look of bafflement on his face. In spite of meeting Blaketon every day in the post office, Clarence never knew his name; in fact, he did not know anyone's name. He never knew mine and I began to wonder if he knew his own or his wife's. He seemed to live blissfully in a world of his own and I began to believe that his head was always full of partially completed inventions. He seemed to be permanently thinking of something to invent. Clarence and Emily lived in a large rambling old house along the Elsinby Road at Aidensfield, and the general appearance of the place mirrored that of Clarence.

Certainly, the house needed a coat of paint, the ivy needed trimming and the hedges could have done with a severe cutting-back. The grounds were extensive, probably approaching a couple of acres, and they were rather untidy too, but he had lots of lovely outbuildings behind the premises. Stone-built with pantile roofs, these were ideal for Clarence because, being artistic, he made things — having made something he would store it in one of his sheds, and then sell it.

I think he had some kind of private income which allowed him to potter about without any kind of urgency or the need for any sort of business acumen, but he was always busy, always out and about, and always somehow successful in selling his handicraft. One of his specialities was concrete garden ornaments. He made gnomes, elves, cats, dogs, tortoises, lizards, squirrels, rabbits, badgers, birds of various kinds and even miniature horse troughs. Sometimes, he would produce a garden bench in concrete, or a bird bath, nesting box or artificial tree stump complete with chopped-off branch-like holes so that blue tits or robins could nest within. His range of concrete garden furnishings grew rapidly — every time he was commissioned to make a particular object, he would produce a copy — the second one becoming part of his increasing stock which he kept for future sale. When a lady wanted a concrete statue of her deceased golden retriever to sit for ever beside her fishpond, for example, Clarence made a pair; when a man wanted the replica of a badger which came to his house for food each evening, he made another and so he accumulated a wonderful array of objects in his numerous sheds.

Although his garden was untidy, his borders full of weeds, his hedges unkempt and his household ivy all enveloping and threatening to darken his windows and doors, his extensive lawn was always well cut by a wonderful machine, on which he doted. It was called a Brott and was a large, motorized petrol-fuelled lawnmower, rather like an invalid carriage in size. The front of the machine sported a seat upon which the operator sat, with a footrest above two small wheels by which the machine could be steered. Steering was affected by a T-shaped handle, while behind the operator's seat was a large collecting area into which the mown grass was propelled for collection in a mesh sack which was carried at the rear. At ground level behind the operator, were the rear wheels and the blades, all encased for safety purposes but driven by a series of belts and pulleys.

The cutting blades could be adjusted for height while the machine was being driven. It could cut very close to the verge in all conditions — long, wet or very thick grass presented no problems. More amazingly, this versatile lawnmower had three forward gears, one reverse and a footbrake. But it was not classified as a motor vehicle because it had been intended only for use on lawns, not roads. Nonetheless, the driver sat at a steering column at the front and, with its gears, brakes and size, it had many of the features of a motor vehicle. However, there were no lights and of course, it did not bear a number plate, nor did it require an excise disc. The likelihood of this particular machine being used on a road was remote in the extreme.

However, nothing is so certain as uncertainty and it so happened that a landscape gardener came to live in Aidensfield and she bought a house with land behind the Anglican church. Her name was Edna Welsh and she required spacious grounds in which to keep her equipment and tools, although most of her work was away from home. Having seen some of Clarence's handiwork, however, she decided she could incorporate his concrete sculptures within some of her designs and so a useful working relationship was established. Wherever possible, she would persuade her clients to include a concrete animal or feature of some kind within their garden design and Clarence would allow her commission on any such sale. However, she did ask that he undertook deliveries of his products to her house — she did not feel able to lift the heavy items on and off her own transport, and for the very heavy work on each site, she hired workmen.

As Clarence lived at one end of Aidensfield and she at the other, he did not have very far to transport his wares. In the main, his other customers took away their own purchases — most of his creations would fit into the rear seat of a family saloon or the back of an estate car — but he did not wish to damage the seats of his personal vehicle. Clarence therefore devised a small, low slung wooden trailer on tiny wheels. It could carry up to four or five concrete life-size badgers and perhaps a squirrel or two and it was precisely right for delivering his creations to Edna Welsh just along the village.

But Clarence had not intended that his trailer be drawn by his car.

For one thing, the trailer was too small, secondly, the towing gear was too low and, thirdly, it was meant to be drawn at very slow speed to prevent its precious load being shaken about or thrown off. Clarence, being of an inventive frame of mind, decided he would hitch it to his Brott. He converted the rear of the lawnmower so that it would accept a draw-bar and thus he had produced a slow-moving delivery vehicle which did not require any kind of licence and which was custom-built for his particular purpose. It was simply a lawnmower with a trailer. Or was it?

Although I did not witness his first few outings (if I had, I would have been duty-bound to question the legality of this arrangement), I do know that Clarence made some successful deliveries to Edna's premises. I had heard he was spreading his creative empire but had no reason to question his methods of delivery. After all, I assumed he would be using some conventional means, even a hand-propelled trolley or barrow of some kind. But then an incident occurred. Police officers generally refer to things as 'incidents' if they are not an accident. This was one of those occasions.

Around five o'clock on spring evening, Clarence had been chugging along the main street of Aidensfield with his Brott and trailer loaded with concrete artefacts. There was a small trough, a bird bath, a pair of ducks, a tortoise, two gnomes with red hats and green jackets and a sleeping bull-dog. All were aboard his trailer, secured where he felt appropriate. He was proceeding along the main street at about five miles an hour when a pair of thirteen-year-old lads, on racing bikes, hurtled out of a gate. He was right in their path — they were lucky he was not driving a steam roller or a heavy goods vehicle.

As they fought to halt their onward rush, each lad skidded on the gravel. One of them collided with Clarence's Brott, and the other rammed his trailer. Both boys were unceremoniously separated from their bikes, both landed heavily in the road and sustained abrasions and cuts, both bicycles suffered minor damage such as scratches and in one case a buckled front wheel and Clarence's trailer was upskittled. Its precious load toppled off, but due to the low height, no damage was caused to either the trailer or its contents, and the Brott was undamaged. In the midst of this kerfuffle, two or three cars screeched to a halt, and because the incident was right outside the post office, ex-Sergeant Blaketon came rushing out to see what was happening. Then he rang me.

'Traffic accident, Nick,' he panted. 'Outside the post office. Three vehicles involved but only slight injuries, ambulance not required.'

'I'll be there in two minutes,' I assured him.

The prospect of a crash between three vehicles in the village street was rather alarming, but when I saw it involved a lawnmower and a couple of pedal cycles, I realised this was not a reportable road traffic accident. It had not occurred due to the presence of a motor vehicle on a road — those were the essential ingredients and there was no motor vehicle here.

As I was taking the names and addresses of everyone involved, our district nurse, Margot Horsfield, appeared, having also been summoned by Oscar Blaketon and she tended the cuts to the boys' knees and hands. I helped Clarence to reload his trailer, the boys said they were otherwise okay, and they could get their bikes home.

As an 'incident', I had all the details and would visit the boys' parents within the next few minutes, just to confirm they were not seriously hurt and to explain what had happened. When everyone had left the scene, Blaketon came over to me and said, 'You're not reporting this, PC Rhea? I see you've not measured the scene . . .'

'It's not a reportable road traffic accident, Oscar,' I almost used his old form of address as Sergeant but restrained myself in time. 'This is not a motor vehicle, it's a lawnmower, and those cycles are not motor vehicles.'

'I would disagree, PC Rhea,' he snapped. 'If I was your supervisory officer . . .'

'You're not,' I smiled.

'But if I was,' he ploughed on. 'I would insist you submitted an accident report. That thing is a motor vehicle and it is on a road; it was on a road when an accident occurred.'

'No, Oscar. That is a lawnmower, it has not been constructed for use on a road and it has not been adapted.'

'It has, it's towing a trailer!'

'The fact it is towing a trailer does not mean it has been adapted for use on a road,' I countered. 'It tows that trailer all over Clarence's premises.'

'I've been watching that thing come up and down the street for the past few weeks, I'll have you know, and for that reason I maintain it has been adapted for use on a road. It's got a petrol engine,' he continued. 'It has four wheels; a driver sits on it and he was guiding it along the road; it has gears and a brake, so in my book that thing, whatever it is, fits the legal definition of a motor vehicle.'

'Remember *Burns v. Currell*, 1963?' I put to him. 'The go-kart case?'

'What about it?' he asked.

'The decision was that in the absence of evidence of regular use on roads, it would seem that the test is whether a reasonable man would contemplate general use of the roads as one of the uses of the vehicle.'

'I am a reasonable man,' he boomed. 'And I have seen that thing making regular use of the roads.'

'And I am a reasonable man, but I think it is a lawnmower,' I said. 'It looks like a lawnmower; it works like a lawnmower and it is used regularly as a lawnmower. It is not a motor vehicle for these purposes, Oscar.'

'If I was your sergeant . . .' he repeated.

'Which you are not, as I have just reminded you—'

'Well, I would order you to submit a report!'

'What kind of report?' I challenged.

'A road accident report, what else?'

'It's not a reportable accident.' I found myself going around in circles with this argument. 'But because it is not a reportable accident, I shall submit an incident report, just to ensure the matter is recorded.'

'You young constables do as you like these days,' he muttered. 'I don't know what things are coming to . . . in my day that would have been an accident, and that thing would have been a motor vehicle because it's got an engine and it's being used on the road.'

'You cannot designate this as a road accident when no motor vehicle has been involved,' I said. 'I'm not going to argue, Oscar, that's my decision.'

'Well, I don't know what your new sergeant will say about all this.'

'Grass cutters are specially exempted, Sergeant.'

'Only those controlled by a pedestrian, Rhea! If the person in control rides on the machine, it could be a motor vehicle.'

'Yes, but only if it is constructed or adapted for use on the roads,' I said. 'This one isn't — it has no lights.'

'Then it should have!'

'Look, I will submit my incident report to Sergeant Craddock and I'll let you know what he says.'

'Right.'

I made a written report of the occurrence and sent it to Craddock at Ashfordly Police Station and was not surprised when he called me.

'Ah, PC Rhea,' his Welsh accent was very prominent over the telephone. 'This incident in Aidensfield main street, the collision between the two cycles and the grass-cutting machine. Would you say that machine was a motor vehicle? It might even qualify as a goods vehicle, you know, seeing it was being used to deliver goods.'

'Ex-Sergeant Blaketon seemed to think it was a motor vehicle, Sergeant.' I smiled as I spoke into the telephone.

'Blaketon? What has he got to do with all this?'

'It was outside his post office. He came out to see what was going on and said I should submit a road traffic accident report.'

'Did he now? Well, in that case, I disagree. I do not think that lawnmower is a motor vehicle, PC Rhea, even if it has been used on a road.'

'Very good, Sergeant.'

And so the report was submitted, but the inspector asked Sergeant Craddock why the lawnmower was not considered a motor vehicle, and then the superintendent asked the inspector the same question, and finally the superintendent's secretary told me that the Accident Prevention Department had asked the superintendent why he had authorised the report to be submitted as an incident, and not an accident.

'Because it was an incident,' he'd said. 'Nothing more than a minor incident in the cheerful daily life of Aidensfield. We don't want that sort of thing cluttering our road traffic accident statistics, do we? And most certainly I am not going to have my officers rebuked or made fun of for charging a man with driving a lawnmower without due care and attention!'

And he'd slammed down the telephone.

CHAPTER 6

One of the great unsolved mysteries of life is why some women do not wish to reveal, or even bear the appearance of, their genuine age. Police officers are aware of this social phenomenon and tend to settle for 'over 21' when recording an interview with a mature woman, although if a lady is asked to produce her driving licence, then her age is conveniently revealed upon it in a coded figure. Police officers know how to interpret that code — which also reveals whether the licence holder is male or female. This helps when the holder has a less than common name, or even in cases where, for example, the holder's name is Hilary or Evelyn. We should not forget that Shirley Crabtree was the name of a very famous and very large male heavyweight wrestler, otherwise known as Big Daddy, but if there was doubt about his masculinity, his driving licence would reveal the truth! This means that on those occasions when a woman has to produce her driving licence, she cannot hide from officialdom's inquisitiveness.

In my time as the constable of Aidensfield, however, driving licences did not contain that code, but whenever we formally interviewed or interrogated women for whatever reason, we had to make a note of their date of birth. We were reprimanded by the sergeant if we did not do so — such details were considered important, usually for statistical purposes. Apart from that, we had to distinguish, for example, between Mrs Amelia Brocklehurst junior and Mrs Amelia Brocklehurst senior should any future dispute be likely. We had to be sure we were dealing with the right person and a date of birth is always a critical factor in making a positive identification.

Inevitably, some ladies objected — and continue to object — to our supposed invasion of their privacy but if, when I was serving, we encountered a particularly objectionable woman who refused to give her age on request, we would add ten years — and we would tell her we were doing so. We'd say our estimation would be entered into the records and that was usually sufficient to persuade her to co-operate by revealing her secret. And most young officers would then switch on the charm and say she did not look anything like her age.

It might be argued that the age of a woman is of no consequence for most of the events in her life — some even conceal their age from their loved ones and work colleagues. Indeed, on most of the occasions a woman seeks help from the police, her age is of no concern — most of the time, we are simply not interested. Clearly, it doesn't matter if she is reporting the loss of a handbag or ringing to say there's a cat stuck up a tree, but we might be interested if her car collided with a pillar box and the question of her fitness to drive became a factor. After all, the reactions of a woman of twenty-one may differ considerably from one of seventy-one. If a woman is arrested for shoplifting, her age may be a factor in the punishment meted out by the court. What all this means, of course, is that there are some occasions when a police officer requires the exact age of the woman with whom he is dealing, and there are other occasions when he does not.

But, for reasons best known to themselves, some women will go to extreme lengths to conceal their true age.

We had a wonderful example of this in Aidensfield. It all began with research into Aidensfield's history and a debate about an oak tree, a species noted for the mighty age it can achieve. The research was undertaken by one of the newcomers to Aidensfield, Clement Baldwin, who was a retired history teacher from Wakefield in the West Riding of Yorkshire. He discovered the former existence of the Aidensfield Oak. It had grown in the centre of the village green and, reputedly, reached the magnificent age of 700 years or thereabouts. It equalled the age of the splendid Lizzie's Oak (Queen Elizabeth's Oak) in Greenwich Park, and Clement's researches showed that it had been in a fine state of health in 1768. By 1868, however, it had died, although its tall, thick stump had remained. Some twenty-five feet high, the stump was smothered in ivy and the parish council had enclosed it within an iron fence to deter dogs and humans who might try to climb it or carve their initials upon its fragile remains. By 1936, however, no trace of the tree remained. Clement could not find out what fate had befallen it, but he felt it would be a wonderful gesture to replace the famous Aidensfield Oak with an infant of the species, planted as near as possible to the original site. He put the idea to the parish council who enthusiastically agreed and so the necessary arrangements began. A sapling would be obtained, it would be planted within secure railings to which would be attached a plaque providing the date of its planting. A further idea was that the oldest resident of Aidensfield would be invited to officially plant the tree which would, over the coming years, become a focal point for the village.

But who was the oldest resident?

The man with access to such personal secrets was Oscar Blaketon because his post office dispensed old age pensions to certain residents, but that kind of information was highly confidential and not for release to the general public. I knew Blaketon would never reveal such information, not even for an occasion as important as the replanting of the Aidensfield Oak. It seemed that identification of the oldest resident would depend upon local knowledge, albeit with some form of later confirmation by the individual concerned.

Members of the parish council exercised their minds on this matter and word spread that they were seeking that person for the historic tree-planting ceremony — they stressed that such a person would have to be currently living in Aidensfield, and also that they must have lived in the village for the whole of their life. This criteria eliminated several who had come to Aidensfield in their retirement and who might otherwise have qualified — there was one old chap of ninety-seven who'd arrived only three years ago from York and a lady of ninety-two who had been a civil servant in London, but it was felt the official tree-planter should be a genuine Aidensfieldonian.

Some discreet research among those with long memories produced two likely candidates, Doris Redfearn and Constance Whittaker. Both had been born in Aidensfield; both had attended the village school; both had been married in the village; both had lived there all their lives; both were still alive and in possession of their faculties; both were widows, and although their exact ages were unknown to most, they were thought to be around the eighty to eighty-five age bracket. They were the obvious candidates, but there was a problem — they hated one other.

They did not speak and neither had a good word to say about the other. Happily, they lived at opposite ends of the village. Doris thought Constance was a complete fool, and Constance thought Doris was a loose woman, a consort of the devil. This antagonism was thought to have resulted from some incident in the dim and distant past, but no one was really sure what had prompted their mutual hostility. Having discovered these two stalwarts, however, the question then arose — which of them was the elder?

In the early stage of this scheme, the parish council did not feel it right to ask either of them outright — discretion was considered important during the weeks of preliminary planning. I tended to agree with this although, as the village constable, I had no official role to play in the proceedings. However, I did assure the organizers I would make myself available for crowd control and traffic regulation during the planting ceremony, and for any other purpose. Like all villagers, I was discreetly asked if I had any information about the actual dates of birth of Doris and Constance, but I hadn't. Neither had been involved in any police matter for which I could demand their dates of birth and I could not add to the debate except to say that, in my opinion, they looked to be about the same age. I offered that opinion bearing in mind that Constance dressed more smartly than Doris and Doris's hair always looked less grey than Constance's. Others had come to a like conclusion and the apparent similarity in their ages raised the possibility that they might be asked to jointly plant the tree. However, their widely broadcast antagonism militated against that suggestion.

After much discussion, the conclusion was that only one of them should plant the tree — and the honour must go to the elder. Further discreet approaches were made to Oscar Blaketon, but he maintained he could not divulge such personal information — he wouldn't even confirm that one was older than the other. I wasn't sure whether records of the type we required were maintained by the Registrar of Births, Marriages and Deaths in nearby Strensford. Inspection of the records could be made, upon payment of a fee, and records in the General Register Office at Somerset House, London were another option. It was decided that our parish could not afford to send someone to London on such a minor errand. A search of the records at Strensford seemed to be one option, if the parish council could legitimately produce the necessary fee, but public scrutiny of the accounts might consider that such expenditure — prying into personal lives — was not in keeping with the spirit of a parish council. However, before that line of approach was debated, news of the parish council's dilemma reached the ears of the respective ladies and Doris Redfearn was first to come forward. She was the widow of a farm worker and even now kept a few hens and ducks, the eggs from which she sold in the shop or to callers at her door. In her old coat and mucky wellies, she went to see the chairman of the parish council, the auctioneer Rudolph Burley.

'Ah've heeard all aboot that tree planting, Mr Burley,' she said, 'and Ah's t'eldest by a good two years. Born in 1879 Ah was, April 5th. Yon Whittaker woman's nobbut a lass compared wi' me. So you'll be expecting me to polish me spade and find summat nice to wear? Wellies is mebbe a good idea?'

'1879, eh? That makes you eighty-seven?'

'Not a day younger! And still as wick as weasel.'

'Well, Doris, you've solved a problem for us. We weren't sure who was the elder.'

'It's not yon Whittaker woman, if that's what you're thinking!'

'Right. And you are absolutely sure you are the oldest resident?'

'Ah should know that, Mr Burley, Ah've lived here all me life!'

'Right, well, thanks for coming forward. I'll report this to the next parish council meeting, then we'll fix a date for the ceremony. I'll be in touch with you about the arrangements when everything's been settled.'

'Does it mean Ah'll get me picture in t'paper?'

'I think that will be very likely,' he'd told her.

'By gum, that will cap yon Whittaker woman . . . Ah'm really keen on this . . . it's usually t'Queen who plants trees, isn't it? Wiv a silver spade.'

'We did ask her to come, but she's very busy running the country and she thought somebody more local would be a better idea,' Rudolph joked.

'Well, next time you're talking wiv her, you can tell her Ah'll do a reet good job on it, so she needn't worry her head about dealing wiv oor tree.'

'I'll do that,' Rudolph promised her. 'And don't you worry about finding a spade, the council will make all the plans and provide all the necessary items. You won't even have to dig the hole, just toss in a spadeful of earth.'

'Is that all? Ah mean, Ah's quite capable of digging an 'ole deep enough for a tree, Mr Burley, and dropping it in, then wattering it. Ah can do a proper job.'

'No, all you'd have to do is turn up on the day and make a token gesture of covering the roots with soil. It's very simple.'

'Fair enough, Mr Burley. So you'll get in touch? About a date and time?'

'We will.'

'And that Whittaker woman won't get a look in?'

'If you are the oldest resident, it will be your privilege, Doris.'

It was a few days later when Rudolph came to see me prior to fixing the tree-planting date. His proposed date was Sunday, 29 May at 2.30 p.m., appropriately enough Oak Apple Day. This date commemorated the time King Charles II had concealed himself in an oak tree at Biscobel in Shropshire after his defeat at Worcester; the tree became known as The Royal Oak and for many years afterwards, celebrations were held nationwide. In Yorkshire, sprigs of oak were worn, church services were held, and boys collected nettles with which to sting the bare legs of young girls — if they did not run away. In Yorkshire, therefore, it was, and still is, known as Nettle Day.

'I am on duty that Sunday,' I told him after checking my diary. 'I'll make sure I'm available to attend — not that there'll be much traffic or a large crowd. But I will arrange some "No Parking" signs for the vicinity of the ceremony.'

'Thanks. We hope to make it a memorable day,' he said. 'There'll be tea in the village hall afterwards, and we might be able to find some twigs of oak for the children. It might encourage the villagers to make an annual ceremony of remembering Oak Apple Day as well as Aidensfield Oak Tree Day.'

'A nice idea,' I said.

'I hope there won't be any trouble,' he smiled. 'During the ceremony, I mean.'

'Trouble?' I puzzled. 'What sort of trouble?'

'Well,' he frowned, 'I've had a visit from Constance Whittaker. She reckons she's the oldest resident, not Doris. She was most upset to learn that Doris was going to do the honours and get her name on the plaque. Constance thought she should have been chosen; she sees herself as a kind of unofficial queen of Aidensfield. I'm sure she's got delusions of grandeur, and she is a bit snooty, but if she is the eldest . . .'

'So how old is she?' I asked.

'She wouldn't say. All she said was that she's older than Doris.'

'She does look older than Doris.' I conjured up a mental picture of Constance in her finery. She was the widow of a successful Ashfordly solicitor who used to specialise in income tax matters, his skills taking him all over the country. He had died about five years ago. With a very smart accent, Constance was a tall, stately woman who favoured fur coats, elaborate hats, high-heeled shoes and afternoon tea in smart hotels and restaurants.

She had always refused to wear spectacles or use a walking stick and looked more like a duchess from Belgravia than a countrywoman. Age was something she had always carefully concealed — but now she had admitted being older than Doris. I got the impression Rudolph had doubts about her claim.

'You're not convinced?' I put to him.

'Well, four years ago we arranged an outing for the over-eighties, it was a special entertainment in the Spa at Scarborough, a 1920s evening, a bit of nostalgia. Over-eighties came from all over Yorkshire, but Constance refused to join us because she said she wasn't eighty then. Doris came, because she was over eighty at the time. In remembering that outing, Doris must be the elder. She should plant the tree.'

'But if Constance won't say exactly how old she is, how can you be sure?'

'Well, surely the onus is on Constance, isn't it? If she's claiming to be older than Doris, then she should provide the necessary proof,' said Rudolph. 'I do find it all rather odd, Constance claiming to be the elder. I think she's after a place in history, wanting her name on the oak tree plaque. I think she's rewriting history to suit her own purposes!'

'You could be right,' I agreed. 'You'll have to persuade both of them to show their birth certificates or provide some other proof.'

'I daren't ask Constance to do that! She's most indignant that anyone should wish to know her real age even if she is claiming to be the elder.'

'You can't accept her word alone, you need proof.' I could see trouble ahead if this event was irregular in any way.

'You're right, but I'm sure her notion of having superior social status has a lot to do with it.'

'You've tried asking Blaketon?' I put to him. 'To settle it out of court, in a manner of speaking?'

'He refuses to get involved; he feels that if he reveals their age, Constance could cause trouble by writing to the newspapers, or her MP or even the post office, to complain about a breach of confidentiality.'

'There must be some way of finding out,' I spoke almost to myself. 'There's always the registrar, either at Strensford or in Somerset House.'

'You have to pay fees to look at the older records,' he told me. 'Anything more than five years old costs money. I doubt if the parish council would authorise that kind of expenditure, and most certainly, it would not sanction a trip to London! Then, of course, there's also the time involved. Checking back through old records can take ages, even with modern indexing systems. That could be our last resort, but truthfully, I don't have that kind of spare time.'

'The information will be held somewhere,' I said. 'It's a case of knowing where to look.'

'Right. Maybe you could do a little investigating for us?' he put to me. 'It's your job, isn't it? Digging for information in all sorts of obscure places . . . maybe you could come up with some ideas to solve this one?'

'Isn't that known as passing the buck?' I grinned.

'Delegation is a better word,' he returned. 'You might even persuade Blaketon to bend his rules and give you their dates of birth.'

'I'll see what I can do,' I said, not very hopefully.

It was a few days later when I popped into the post office to buy some stamps and, as there was no one else on the premises at the time, I asked Blaketon,

'You know the tree-planting ceremony in May . . .' I began.

'If you think I'm going to divulge the birth dates of people in this village, Nick, you've another think coming! You're not the first to ask, but I can't breach our rules of confidentiality, you know that.'

'Sorry I asked!' I grinned ruefully.

I began to wonder how we could unearth the dreaded birth dates of the two battling ladies. I did think I might go to the village school to ask for a look at their very old records, and then there were newspaper files which might have records of births, deaths and marriages. I shrank from examining the old records in Aidensfield school because if I did, word of my actions would circulate in the village and, sure as shot, it would reach both Doris and Constance. They would know I did not believe their claims, and that I was fishing for snippets of information — and I did not wish to even hint I disbelieved either of them.

Then I had a brainwave. It happened as I was walking along the village street early one evening; I was in civilian clothes and off duty, on my way to post a birthday card. I met Clement Baldwin as he was on his way for an early pre-dinner drink at the Brewers' Arms. It was the sight of Clement which produced my idea.

He was a tall, smartly dressed man with a very slim figure, a mop of white hair with no sign of baldness, and very healthy pink cheeks beneath gold rimmed spectacles.

'Clement,' I said. 'Mind if I join you for a drink? I'd like to pick your brains.'

'You'll have a job to find my brain, Nick, let alone pick it,' he chuckled. 'I've retired, you know.'

'It's about the oak tree planting,' I said.

'Right, I'm all yours,' and he led the way into the bar. I ordered a couple of pints and we settled in a quiet corner with our drinks. We chatted about nothing in particular until he asked, 'So, what is it you want to ask?'

I referred to the tree planting, a subject dear to his heart, and then told him about the dilemma concerning Doris and Constance. He listened carefully, then clarified his own mind by saying, 'So Doris claims she is the eldest at eighty-seven, while Constance makes a similar claim, but she won't give you any idea of her age? And you can't get proof of either?'

'We can, but not very easily; it involves time and expense.'

'So what can I do?' he frowned.

'You're still researching the history of Aidensfield,' I said.

'I am.'

'I wondered if you were examining the school records? Or delving into old newspaper files. That sort of thing.'

'Well, yes, it's all part of my on-going research, Nick. How does that help?'

'Well, I wondered if either Doris or Constance was mentioned in the school records, their surnames would be different of course, but it occurred to me that it might be one way of determining their true ages. And if their births were in the papers of the time, or their marriages . . .'

'Got it!' he said. 'As a matter of fact, I do have the school attendance registers at home right now, going back years, and some other books. I have permission to examine the local newspaper library whenever I am free. If both these ladies are around eighty, it gives me a starting point. Right, Nick, Operation Ageless Lady begins as of tonight. I'll get in touch when I have some news. We've a few weeks yet, haven't we?'

'Yes, time's still on our side. But you'll be discreet?'

'In dealing with the sensitive issue of a woman's age? Of course!'

We had another drink then he left to go home while I made my way to the hilltop police house.

Some ten days later, I received a telephone call from Clement. He announced he had located the information and suggested we went for a quiet walk, out of earshot, to discuss his findings. I felt this had all the hallmarks of a Secret Service meeting — absolutely right for such a momentous matter. We walked along the ridge behind Aidensfield which afforded panoramic views across the landscape with the evening sun highlighting some of the features. We could see the becks, the roads, houses in remote places, the patchwork of fields, the church towers rising in the dale — it was a most pleasant excursion.

When we were some distance from the village, Clement said, 'I have a surprise for you, Nick, or perhaps for the parish council,' and he smiled. 'Who do you think is the oldest of those two?'

'I'm now putting my money on Doris. If Doris says she's eighty-seven, I'm inclined to believe her. Even though Constance looks the sort who would knock years off her true age, I doubt if she's that old. I think she's after some kind of local glory.'

'They're the same age,' he chuckled. 'I have an old school register; both were born on 4 April 1883, in Aidensfield, and both started school on the same day. And both their surnames were Potter. They're cousins, Nick. First cousins. So there we are. One might be a few hours older than the other, but when it comes to planting oak trees, I'd say they were the same age.'

'So that makes them both eighty-three?' I did a quick mental calculation. 'Not eighty-seven?'

'Right,' he smiled. 'And their births are recorded in the *Ashfordly Herald*. That paper's defunct now, but they've got copies in the county library. Two family notices, Nick. All good social history for me. And one source confirms the other.'

'I'd better tell Rudolph,' I said. 'It's his problem now.'

'Either you plant two oak trees, or you get both ladies to plant the same one.'

'Sparks will surely fly if we do that!' I suggested.

'And we would not want our brand-new oak tree to be burnt to the ground by sparks from feuding old ladies, would we?'

'Joking aside, Clement, why would a woman add years to her age? Doris has told us she's eighty-seven but in fact she's four years younger than that! Why on earth would she do that? I thought they knocked years off their ages, not added to them!'

'Who can understand the mind of a woman?' Clement smiled. 'You'll have to ask her, Nick. So there you are, a slice of local history for you and your parish council.'

We returned to the village where I bought him a drink and we parted with me promising I would relay the result of his research to Rudolph Burley. Rudolph, I learned, was in Newcastle-on-Tyne at some kind of conference involving auctioneers and he was not expected back in Aidensfield until Monday — it was Friday when I talked to Clement. But the date of the planting was still some time away and I could wait. But Constance hailed me in the village on the Sunday morning as I was leaving mass.

'Ah, Constable Rhea,' she said in her haughty voice. 'Just the man.'

'Yes, Mrs Whittaker, what can I do for you?'

'I fear there is to be a case of false pretences in Aidensfield if you are not careful.' Her face was rigid and unsmiling. 'I think you ought to know about it and then do something to prevent a dreadful miscarriage of public trust.'

'False pretences?' I puzzled.

'That Redfearn creature from the far end of the village,' and her nose rose into the air like a pointer sniffing for a scent.

'Doris? What's happened?'

'She is claiming to be the oldest resident of Aidensfield, Constable Rhea, and it is totally untruthful. I am the oldest resident, and it is I who should be planting that oak tree for posterity. Not her.'

'She says she is eighty-seven,' I told her. 'So how old are you?'

'My age is nothing to do with this, Constable Rhea; all I am saying is that I am older than that woman and that, surely, is what counts.'

I looked at Constance, still a fine woman in spite of her years, and I decided it was time to reveal my own knowledge.

'Mrs Whittaker,' I said. 'I happen to know that you and Mrs Redfearn are the same age. You are cousins, you were born on the same day in 1883 which makes you both eighty-three.'

'Maybe that is so, Constable Rhea.' She did not blink an eyelid at my revelation. Her self-control was remarkable. 'But the fact remains, I am still the eldest, even if it is only by six hours.'

'Six hours?'

'Six hours, Constable Rhea. I am six hours older than that Redfearn woman and that is what counts, not our calendar age.'

'If you are as close together as that, I can't see it matters so far as planting oak trees is concerned. You are the same age, you share the same birthday, but it is a matter for the parish council. I suspect that they will need proof, Mrs Whittaker, of your age and that of Mrs Redfearn, but in my view the sensible thing is to share the planting ceremony!'

'Share a public platform with that woman? I shall do no such thing! But my purpose in speaking to you is to remind you that you represent the law in Aidensfield. I wish to state my case for being the rightful person to perform that ceremony. '

'I shall mention it to the parish council,' I assured her.

'And so you shall, Constable. There must be no fraudulent claims in matters of this kind. We are talking history here, PC Rhea, permanent records, that sort of thing. Rightfulness must prevail!'

'Rudolph Burley is chairman of the parish council, he's in charge of the arrangements,' I stressed. 'Perhaps you'd like to talk to him personally?'

'Perhaps I shall because I do not wish my age to be mentioned. You are the police; you are privy to secrets and know how to remain silent on important issues. If I claim to be a mere seventy-nine, due to my youthful appearance, it is no concern to anyone else. All that needs saying on the planting day is that I am the oldest resident of Aidensfield, nothing more. And I am the oldest resident, Constable Rhea. That is the point — the only point — that I am making.'

'In view of what you have told me, I am sure you are right, Mrs Whittaker. Shall I tell Rudolph to expect you? He is away at the moment, he's due back on Monday.'

'I expect you to brief him about this conversation, but I shall see him myself as you suggest. But if that man Blaketon has been revealing any of my personal particulars, I shall complain to the postal authorities, Constable Rhea.'

'He hasn't, Mrs Whittaker, Mr Blaketon is highly trustworthy in all matters of confidentiality. I can assure you of that. All the relevant information is in public records if you know where to look — locally, that's old newspapers, school registers, that kind of thing.'

Her face fell; her jaw dropped, and she looked ten years older in a matter of a fraction of a second. 'You mean people could know about all this, people who should not know?'

'No, I am sure your secret is safe, Mrs Whittaker. I'm sure they do not know because I am sure no one's taken the trouble to do that kind of research. But if anyone really wants to delve into the history of this village — and you are part of it — then the information is freely available.'

'This is dreadful. I had no idea people could pry into one's personal matters . . . but I am six hours older than that other woman, Constable Rhea. But if public records are available, my claim can be substantiated. Six hours — it makes such a difference! Remember that as I plant my tree!'

And she stomped away. She had style, I felt; I thought I should have complimented her on the manner of her conversation, but I would pass the information to Rudolph upon his return. It looked as if he had a major decision to make. In all fairness to Doris, however, I felt she ought to be aware of this development and so I popped in to see her. She made me welcome, a pot of tea had just been made and she invited me to join her with a scone and some strawberry jam. I did so.

'Doris,' I said. 'I've been doing a spot of research into local history, me and Clement Baldwin, that is.'

'And?'

'We've seen the school records, when you and Constance started. Doris Potter and Constance Potter, cousins. Sharing the same birthday. You're the same age, Doris, aren't you? You are not eighty-seven as you claim, you're only eighty-three.'

She did not reply for a long time then said, 'It had to come out sometime, Ah suppose. Does that mean Ah'll not be planting that tree?'

'That's a matter for the parish council to decide, Doris. With the pair of you sharing a birthday, it might mean other arrangements have to be made.'

'Ah'm not sharing with that Whittaker woman, and that's final!' snapped Doris. 'You can tell that to your council.'

'Is she right, though, about being six hours older than you?'

'No, it's me that's t'oldest, Mr Rhea. Ah'm six hours older than her.'

'Oh crumbs,' I groaned. 'Here we go again! Who can prove that?'

'Only our mothers, and they're not around anymore,' grinned Doris. 'When we were born, we were born at home and nobody worried about t'exact time. The midwife went from house to house and she came to our house first. Ah remember me mother telling me Ah was born afore Constance. So it's me who's older than yon Whittaker woman.'

'I'll have to tell the council . . .'

'It's allus happened like this, her getting all t'good jobs. Ever since Ah was at school with that woman, she allus got t'best things to do, t'best desk in t'school, number one coat hanger, all t'best jobs in t'bakery lessons, captain of rounders, pencil monitor . . . all because she talks posh . . .'

'Is that why you added a few years to your age?' I smiled.

'Aye, Ah did, so Ah could start smoking afore her, have drinks in t'pub, get boyfriends and things. When folks thought Ah was t'eldest by a year or two, they started looking up to me . . . after Ah'd left school, that was.'

'And you kept up the pretence?'

'Aye, not even me 'usband, God bless 'im, knew me real age, and Ah never applied for a driving licence or owt like that, so Ah didn't 'ave to let on.'

'Well, I think you should be honest with Rudolph now.'

'Oh aye, Ah will, because Ah'm t'eldest anyroad which means Ah can still plant yon tree?' And I could see the smile of triumph on her face. Then I left.

There was a momentary lull in hostilities during the weekend and my instincts told me that the two tree-planting ladies were lying in ambush for Rudolph. I learned that each had been to his house on Monday morning, demanding that his wife let it be known that Doris and Constance each claimed his attention before the other. By chance, I was passing on my morning patrol and Mrs Burley hailed me.

'I've had those two battling battle-axes hammering on my door, Mr Rhea.' Jane Burley was rounded and jolly, with a head of dark brown hair which belied her fifty or so summers. 'They said you'd discovered they were the same age, and each demands to know who's going to plant the tree.'

'Can you contact Rudolph before he gets home?' I asked.

'He said he would ring me from Scotch Corner; that gives me an hour or so to have a meal ready when he gets in.'

'If I were you, I'd alert him to this development,' I said. 'He might wish to think things through before he gets here. Or come home through the back door!'

'I'll tell him,' she smiled.

Within a couple of hours, however, Jane Burley was ringing my house and because I was out on patrol, Mary, my wife, contacted Ashfordly Police Station with the result that Alf Ventress hailed me on my Mini-van radio.

'Nick,' he said after the radio formalities. 'It seems there is some kind of a picket-line outside Rudolph Burley's house in Aidensfield. Two elderly woman are there, one at each side of his garden gate, awaiting his return from a meeting. Mrs Burley says it's beginning to look confrontational and she fears trouble — can you attend?'

'Will co,' I said. Ten minutes later I was easing to a halt outside the house and sure enough, Doris and Constance were stationed at either side of Rudolph's garden gate, each with arms folded and fierce expressions on their faces. Neither was looking at the other for both were staring stony-faced into the road, awaiting Rudolph.

'Look,' I addressed them both from a position of safety in the middle of that quiet road. 'Rudolph's not back yet, he'll see you both when he returns . . .'

'I'm the rightful planter!' snapped Constance. 'I want Mr Burley to know that!'

'Don't be daft, Ah'm t'right one!' came in Doris.

'Look,' I said, 'if there is trouble here, I'll have you both in court for conduct likely to cause a breach of the peace and that'll mean neither of you will plant the tree.'

'You'll make criminals out of us?' snapped Constance. 'This smacks of a police state, the heavy hand of the law being brought down on a defenceless woman.'

'Two defenceless women!' said Doris.

'Two defenceless old women!' added Constance.

I thought the latter comment might have been an ice-breaker, but I realised I needed something capable of melting the polar ice-caps. As each woman turned her face away from the other, I noticed Clement Baldwin heading towards us. He was looking his usual cheerful self, but his expression changed to one of alarm when he realised that a reception committee awaited Rudolph.

'Something wrong?' he asked, as he approached the vigilantes of the gate.

'Not wrong,' I smiled at him. 'These ladies wish to speak to Rudolph but he's not back yet.'

'Ah, well, I want to see him too. He is due back soon, isn't he? Not that my purpose is particularly urgent.'

'We're expecting him any moment,' I said. 'And thanks for that information you gleaned from the school records, it has been most useful.'

'So it was you, was it?' snapped Constance. 'Prying into our business!'

'Doing historical research, ladies,' beamed Clement. 'Fascinating stuff, village history. You two started school together,' he continued. 'Like twins, almost. The teacher was proud of you both; I can remember some of the comments she recorded, and you were pals as little girls, then you fell out, eh? After the Miriam Stopford incident.'

'The what?' asked Doris.

'The Miriam Stopford incident,' repeated Clement.

'I know nowt about that!' snapped Doris.

'And neither do I!' added Constance. 'So what was it? What did Miriam do? She left anyway, when we had scarlet fever. Me and Doris, we went down with it at the same time, and when we got back Miriam had left. She started Elsinby school instead, still lived in Aidensfield though. We were only six or seven, so it didn't mean much . . .'

'She tore out some pages from your exercise book, Constance, some English sentences you'd written, and she threw them in the beck . . . they were found later, and she was admonished. The teacher called it the Miriam Stopford incident because it had caused such a fuss.'

'Miriam did that?' Constance looked puzzled and hurt.

'Her parents were most upset that she would be so hurtful. She won the school prize for her English work, she denied you the prize.'

'There you are — Ah told you it wasn't me!' and a wide smile illuminated Doris's face. 'You said it was me; you blamed me all those years and it never was me . . . it was that Miriam.'

'And I asked her to be my bridesmaid! She was my best friend . . .' A look of absolute misery flooded across Constance's face. 'I trusted her and all the time she'd done that . . . nobody told me, Mr Baldwin, nobody. I always thought it was our Doris who'd done that . . . always . . .'

'That's 'cos we were off school for weeks wi' scarlet fever,' Doris nodded. 'It had all blown over by the time we got back, forgotten I shouldn't be surprised.'

'You'd think somebody would have told us!' Constance's face was a picture of deep misery. 'And I blamed you, Doris, all these years, and you sought your revenge because I blamed you and kept having a go at you . . . and oh, dear, I just don't know what to say now.'

To cut a long story short, Rudolph's car turned into the high street during this emotional moment, but we decided not to bother him with this problem just yet. We just waved as he turned down a side lane which would enable him to reach his back door.

Constance said, 'I'm going to put the kettle on, Doris, will you come for tea and a scone?'

'Aye, Ah will,' said Doris.

'And you Mr Rhea? And Mr Baldwin?'

'No, thanks,' we chorused. 'This is for you!'

'I think you should spend some time with each other, you've a lot to talk about,' said Clement.

'Are we rewriting Aidensfield history?' I asked.

'No, just putting the record straight,' he said.

Doris and Constance became friends again after all that time and, together, they planted the Aidensfield Oak.

It stands there today in its collar of protective steel railings which bear a plaque saying:

The Aidensfield Oak. Planted on 29 May 1966, Royal Oak Day, by Doris Redfearn and Constance Whittaker, the longest living residents of the village. This replaces an earlier tree which dates to medieval times.

And there is no reference to their actual age.

CHAPTER 7

Claude Jeremiah Greengrass was one of thousands of dealers throughout the nation who managed to earn a living from buying and selling second-hand goods. I do not include genuine antiques in this scenario, but scrap iron, old household goods, second-hand furnishings, discarded ovens and washing machines, old cars and bicycles, dead cattle and horses, rags and bottles and a mass of other miasma which always seemed to be in demand. It was difficult to imagine why anyone would want to buy such stuff and it is something of a mystery how people managed to earn a living from selling other people's junk. Nonetheless, it has often been said that everything comes in useful once every seven years, but why would anyone buy the sort of rubbish peddled by scrappies — as we called these characters? Their activities did support the long understanding among country people that anything would sell in due course — the rubbish of today becomes the antique of tomorrow, and I think such optimistic philosophy was inbred in second-hand dealers. In spite of everything, their activities must have had some kind of impact upon the national economy because there were items of specially framed legislation designed to cater for their work, and for others in areas of similar enterprise.

A glance at some of the terminology reveals a wonderful array of persons who buy and sell a bewildering array of merchandise — there are scrap-metal dealers, pawnbrokers, pedlars, hawkers, game dealers, knackers, money-lenders, mediums, dealers in securities, mock auctions, medicines, poisons, liquor, food, furniture, bedding, clothing, obscene publications and even assorted verminous articles.

I am sure there are others, such as prostitutes and poachers, whose business activities attract scrutiny from various officials, including the police, but for reasons which never become glaringly obvious. Claude Jeremiah Greengrass, a dealer of considerable local esteem, seemed able to exempt himself from most of the rules governing others of his kind.

Even now, I have little idea how he managed to distance himself from the welter of legal provisions. For example, when the Scrap-Metal Dealers Act of 1964 became effective, he said his premises were not a scrap-metal store; they were a smallholding chiefly concerned with furniture, vegetable produce and livestock. Then, when someone suggested he should obtain a pedlar's licence, he said it did not apply to him because he did not travel on foot exposing for sale his goods, wares or merchandise, and he claimed he was not a hawker because he did not use a horse as a beast of burden.

He maintained that his scruffy dog, Alfred, was not a beast of burden and assured the authorities that he did not deal solely in game, so he was not a game dealer, nor did he lend money at exorbitant interest rates, so he was not a moneylender within the terms of the Money-lenders Act of 1900, then in force. In other words, because Claude Jeremiah dealt with such a wide range of merchandise in very small quantities none of which formed the main thrust of his work, he was able to avoid most forms of registration, licensing and official supervision. I am quite convinced he also managed to avoid scrutiny by the Inland Revenue inspectors by always insisting on cash deals.

His skilful avoidance of formal supervision meant that I kept a watchful eye upon him and his activities, one reason being that stolen property might find its way into his emporium. It was for such a reason that I decided to visit his premises to ascertain whether a load of stolen scrap aluminium had come to his notice.

Details of the theft had been circulated to all police forces in England and Wales, and although my approach to the Greengrass ranch did not highlight any dumped aluminium, I did notice a huge pile of stone slabs. They were heaped on a patch of open moorland close to the lane which led into his ranch, and the pile seemed to comprise thousands of neat, well-cut pieces of York stone.

This kind of handsome stone was always in demand for patios, footpaths, drives and garden areas both in large and small quantities. I am not an expert in the weight of stone, but I estimated there were several tons on Claude's property — but that was not the purpose of my visit. There had been no notice of such a theft, and I was seeking aluminium.

'What is it now?' Greengrass appeared from his doorway even before I had brought my Mini-van to a halt. 'Suspected of some crime, am I? Nothing changes, Constable Rhea. If summat goes missing, Greengrass is the first port of call. Chief suspect I am!'

'Suspected? You, Claude? Who in their right mind would suspect such a fine, upstanding member of the community? I do not suspect you — not at the moment, that is, but a load of aluminium has gone missing from Teesside.'

'Aluminium?' he roared. 'What would I want with a load of aluminium?'

'Who knows?' I returned. 'Good-quality scrap metal of a superior nature is always worth a few quid, especially with no questions asked. I wondered if you'd heard any whispers about it.'

'I have not, and, besides, that's out of my league, Constable. I wouldn't touch it with a bargepole. Old bedsteads, bit of scrap lorries and cars, old girders, derelict bridges and worn-out horseshoes are more in my line. Sorry to disappoint you, but I've seen nowt of a load of aluminium, and I've heard nowt.'

'But you will let me know if it happens to cross your busy path?' I smiled.

'I might,' he grinned, blinking his eyes rapidly. 'You'll have to keep calling back, won't you? Hot information doesn't come cheap. I've a living to earn.'

'I'll be back,' I assured him. 'And I see you've a nice pile of cut stone.'

'Freshly delivered this morning, Constable, from West Yorkshire. A new line for me. York stone, neatly cut and ready to lay — ideal for patios, footpaths, gardens, even kitchen floors in converted barns. It comes a bit expensive when it's as well cut as mine, but I can always arrange a good deal, you know that. Good discount for quantities. And you'll notice I have quite a lot out there, enough to service a few high-class orders. It's a very acceptable load of high-quality stone.'

'So where did you get it?' was my next question.

'Suspicious as always! You blokes never give up, do you? But where I got it is my business! I'm not saying because I might want to go back for more,' he grinned. 'I don't want word of my supplier to reach the opposition — this source is mine and mine alone.'

'And I suppose it is for sale?'

'It is. Why else would it be here? You can sell anything, Constable, anything at all, if the quality's right. And if it puts your mind at rest, it's not been nicked, I can tell you that. I bought it cheap. I outbid the competition. It's good quality York stone and most of it's cut and shaped into very interesting designs. Architects, builders, landscape gardeners and such will love it. You can pass the word around if you like, Constable.'

'Act as your agent, you mean?'

'Unpaid, I hope. You get invited into some very wealthy establishments and you might just drop across someone who's fancying a nice bit of York paving. So point them in my direction, Constable. And they might pass the word around that Greengrass has a large stock of high-quality stone slabs, all bought legitimately. All above board and legal. That's me. And remember, there's a discount for quantity.'

'I'll bear it in mind even if it does sound too good to be true,' I said, secretly concerned about his acquisition of the stone. But as we had received no complaints about such a theft, I accepted his word.

On my way out of his emporium, I stopped to examine the pile of cut stone and was agreeably surprised both by the quantity and quality; each slab was piled on top of another, so I could see only the ends and some sides, not the faces. But from what I could see, some were cut into oblong shapes while others had more decorative tops and sides. I spotted a few curves while looking at a selection of end elevations and could just discern that some had intricate floral designs.

If they were all like those on top of his pile, then each had a smooth expanse of York stone on the upper side, ideal for footpaths and patios, as he had claimed.

'I can arrange for them to be cut to size,' Claude followed me along the lane. 'Any size and shape on request. I can soon get one of those big 'uns cut down to half-size or whatever. You can't beat that for a deal, Constable. Personal service, in other words. So if you want a patio outside Chez Fuzz, just let me know.'

'I'm not allowed to make unauthorised improvements to police property,' I smiled. 'But if I do hear of anyone who's looking for some good slabs of York stone, I'll send them here.'

'I don't pay commission, you know.'

'And I don't accept things at face value, Claude. I'm still curious as to where you obtained those slabs.'

'Don't let it bother you,' he grinned. 'Just say the people involved had no objection to me buying their stones. I've had not one word of complaint, Constable, not one.'

'I am still intrigued,' I said, as I regained my Mini-van and left the Greengrass premises. At home, I searched our regular printed despatches for details of crimes committed throughout the north of England but found no report of stolen York stone slabs. Suspicious as I was, I had to concede that this Greengrass enterprise appeared to be perfectly legal.

It would be a week or so later, during a visit to the home of Mr and Mrs Austin Rigby, who were wealthy residents of Aidensfield, that I was asked if I knew of any dealer who could supply York stone, ready dressed. It seemed that the Rigbys were renovating their home and had decided to install a natural stone floor in their kitchen. They wanted large slabs of dressed York stone, and so I told them about the Greengrass collection. And off they went to have a look. They were suitably impressed and spoke to their builder who also examined the stone; he pronounced it just right for the project and so the deal was done. The builder calculated the quantity required and asked Claude to deliver it to Ivy Cottage, the home of the Rigbys. Within a few days, Claude and his assistant, David Stockdale, were loading slabs into Claude's wheezing old truck and these were duly deposited in the back garden of the Rigby household. They remained until required — as I passed, I counted them. They had been neatly stacked into two piles, one containing thirteen slabs and the other twelve. Clearly, the Rigbys had a large kitchen but it was evident they had selected slabs all of the same size, all oblong with no fancy carvings or curves. I guessed each one was about four feet long by two feet six inches wide.

It was while they were awaiting installation that George Ingram of Ashdale House in Aidensfield noticed them and decided that one slab would be ideal as a backing for the fireplace he was ripping out. He was installing oil-fired central heating in his home and felt he could cheerfully get rid of his sooty old fireplace. If the blackened, specially shaped backplate was removed, it could be replaced by one of Claude's slabs, and his wife could put flowers in the clean new space thus created. So another deal was done.

And then Mrs Daniella Foxton realised a selection of the slabs would be ideal as stepping stones across her lawn — she had just had a goldfish pond installed at the bottom of her garden, and stone slabs set into the grass would enable her to visit her fish without getting her feet wet in dewy conditions. And she did not object to slabs with curved tops or wiggly sides — they would be all the more decorative in her garden design.

In a very short space of time, therefore, Claude's large pile of York stone was fast dwindling as he sold slabs for a variety of projects all over Aidensfield, and instead of his pile being the only one in the district, there were now several piles, some large and some small, with Mr Ingram's being a pile of just one piece. And Claude had delivered the lot.

I encountered Claude in the Brewer's Arms one evening when I was off duty and he bought me a drink — my agency fee — because it had been my chat to Mr and Mrs Rigby which had prompted the demand. Clearly, the Rigbys had been very impressed because they were thinking of building a conservatory with a stone floor, but that project must wait a while. But things began to go wrong. As work started on their new kitchen, I received a phone call from Clare Rigby.

'Mr Rhea,' she said. 'You recommended Mr Greengrass to us, if my memory serves me correctly, for the stone we're using in our kitchen.'

'Yes,' I confirmed. 'I thought it looked ideal for your floor.'

'And so did we, Mr Rhea, but there is a small problem.'

'It's not stolen, is it?' I put to her. 'I did check; there's no record of that stone being illegally obtained. I am sure it is all perfectly legal.'

'I am sure you are right, PC Rhea, but do you know where he obtained those stones?'

'No,' I had to admit. 'We'd had no reports of any theft, so I did not pursue the matter.'

'All those beautiful stone slabs, Mr Rhea, are former gravestones. When I looked at the underside of one of those I had bought, it bore a carved epitaph to someone called Arkwright who died in Bradford. That was the side Claude concealed from us. And when we managed to look at the others, they're all the same — each one of them bears an epitaph in memory of some dear departed person. I am not particularly squeamish, Mr Rhea, but I do not relish the idea of having that kind of message under my kitchen floor. I'd be seeing ghosts all night; I'd be having nightmares about the dear departed, wondering whose grave had been robbed for me to stand my cooker on.'

'They're all gravestones, are they?'

'Yes, I think so, they are all alike or very similar, some are nicely designed, but I haven't been able to look at them all, they're too heavy to move.'

'I don't think Greengrass is a grave robber, Mrs Rigby. I am sure he has obtained them legitimately. We've no reports of thefts from graveyards.'

'I'm sure he has acquired them honestly, Mr Rhea, but I do not want someone's memorial — lots of memorials in fact — under my feet all day . . . I would not feel comfortable. I shall see Mr Greengrass myself; I do not wish you to become involved unless there is a criminal matter to complain about.'

'I don't think there is, Mrs Rigby. He's not made any false representations about the stones — he's just not told his customers where they came from and there's nothing illegal in that.'

'I felt you should know, so you can warn others who might be tempted to buy them. I shall ask Mr Greengrass to recover them, and I shall ask for a refund.'

'I wonder if the other buyers realise this?' I mused.

Clearly, they had not realised the source of their newly acquired stonework and it was Mrs Ingram, upon hearing of the Rigbys' experience, who asked her husband to lift up the stone soon to be installed as their fireback. And on the side lying face down in her back garden, it said:

Here lies the body of Sarah Pickard, much loved wife of Harold and mother of Lily and Annie. Esteemed by all. Born 1779, died 1858. RIP.

'I can't allow that to be used in my living-room!' she said when she spotted me in the village street afterwards. 'I have told Mr Greengrass to remove it immediately, and to return my money. George and I will look out for a nice piece of moorland granite instead.'

The same applied to the others who had purchased pieces of Greengrass stone and so Claude and David found themselves reloading the gravestones.

They were all returned to his ranch for storage. I heard later that he had refunded most of the money, which had originally been paid in cash, although he had managed to retain a little 'for delivery and administration expenses'. And so the great Greengrass gravestone sale was over. I saw him a few days later and he sounded very philosophical about it.

'There's nowt wrong with 'em,' he said. 'No chips, cracks, weaknesses . . . it's just that them folks were a bit squeamish . . .'

'You should have told them, Claude,' I said. 'So where did you get them?'

'There's an old graveyard near Leeds. It's never been used for over a hundred years and the church is redundant, so they're selling it off as building land. The graveyard had to be cleared and I got the job. Nobody wants those stones, folks whose ancestors were known to be there were approached, and some re-erected the stones in new spots, but all these, all these in my drive, they're all unwanted.'

'So what now?' I asked.

'They'll sell,' he sounded confident. 'Everything sells in the due course of time. Somewhere, someday, a chap will come along and want that pile of gravestones. They'll take no harm there. They've lasted over a hundred years already and they'll last another hundred. And I've made a few bob out of them anyroad. No harm done.'

I did wonder whether the stones would be broken up to form a base for someone's drive or patio, but that would be a shame because they were beautifully dressed and splendidly coloured. I began to wonder if I would mind if they formed the floor to a patio or conservatory, epitaph-side down, but had to concede that I might not be entirely happy with the idea. As the weeks passed, the saga of the gravestones faded in my memory although the pile beside Greengrass's drive did not diminish — it seemed no one wished to buy them.

And then I received a note from Leicestershire Police to the effect that a gentleman called James Rodwell had moved from an address in Leicestershire to Chapel Howe at Shelvingby, on the edge of my beat. The reason for the correspondence was that Mr Rodwell was the holder of a firearm certificate and I was being notified that he had moved on to my patch. He would have to submit his certificate to my chief constable, through me, for our records to be updated. My task was to give him a gentle reminder, while at the same time inspecting his firearms to ensure they agreed with those recorded on the certificate.

The following day, therefore, I drove out to Shelvingby, a hillside village on the edge of the moors but when I arrived, I realised I did not know the whereabouts of Chapel Howe. I popped into the shop and asked.

'Oh, it's the Methodist Chapel, Mr Rhea,' smiled Mrs Hollins, the shop keeper. 'Since the congregation dwindled to nowt, it's been sold and that chap, Rodwell, is converting it into a house. It's along the lane behind this shop, you can't miss it.'

'Thanks.'

It was the work of a moment to locate the former chapel and, when I arrived, the place was ringing to the sound of hammering and drilling. Clouds of dust emanated from the open windows, and I saw two builders' vans in what had been the parking area of the former chapel. Shouting an advance warning, I approached the door just as a youthful, dark-haired man was emerging.

'Oh! The law!' He stopped dead in his tracks as he shouted. 'What's this, Constable? Somebody complaining about the noise?'

'No, nothing like that. I had no idea you were in the middle of all this . . . I thought you'd moved in.' And I explained the letter from Leicestershire Police.

'I'm camping here, I've got a camp bed and a Primus stove until this lot's finished, and my wife is at her mother's; the furniture is in storage and the dog's in kennels. And if it's my firearms certificate you're wanting, that's in storage as well. I reckon it'll take another three weeks before it's looking like home.'

'No problem,' I assured him. 'We can deal with it when you're settled in.'

'I'd offer you a cup of tea, but I've only got one mug,' he grinned. 'And those builders have their own.'

'No, I don't want to hinder you. I'll come back in a week or two, when things are more settled.'

'Fine,' he smiled. 'But look, are you local?'

'I am,' I said. 'PC Rhea, I'm based at Aidensfield and this is part of my beat.'

'Right, then you'll be just the chap to tell me where I can get a load of nice York stone slabs, I want to lay a forecourt after I've knocked a doorway in the south wall. These builders can't help, they're not local, they're from Middlesbrough.'

'I know where there's a pile of beautiful York stone slabs,' I smiled. 'Enough to build a unique wall around your garden as well as make a patio!'

'Brilliant!' he smiled. 'Enough for a wall, you say? That's just what I want.'

'There is a problem,' I had to tell him. 'They're all former gravestones, complete with inscriptions and, in some cases, decorative designs.'

'You're joking?'

'I'm not.' And I explained their whereabouts with due emphasis upon the personage of one Claude Jeremiah Greengrass.

'Look, I've got to get over there right now, I don't want to lose these,' he said. 'I want some old gravestones, as many as I can get, to build into the walls around the garden, where the dry, stone walls have tumbled or been nicked, and I can replace some of the worn stone in the chapel walls. I mean, what better stones could you have for a former chapel?'

'And the fact they have inscriptions on them doesn't bother you?'

'On the contrary, that's just how I want them, for atmosphere.'

He explained that, although he was converting the interior of the chapel into a comfortable modern home, he wanted the outside to retain its former appearance and appeal. There had been no graveyard at the chapel — burials had been arranged in the local Anglican churchyard — but he felt that if old gravestones were incorporated by standing upright against the outer walls and in the garden walls, then they would both honour those mentioned in the epitaphs and at the same time complement the appearance of the former place of worship.

Even as I was leaving, he was shaking dust from his clothes and heading for his car. 'Thanks, Constable,' he said.

And a couple of days later, Claude Jeremiah Greengrass bought me another drink as he said, 'Things will allus sell, Constable Rhea, provided they're good enough. Now, do you know anybody who wants to buy a ship's propeller or a stuffed horse?'

* * *

One of the more puzzling pieces of legislation, particularly in the minds of sceptical people like police officers, was the Fraudulent Mediums Act of 1951; such scepticism arose because many felt that *all* mediums, especially tricksters who reckoned they could converse with the spirits of one's dear departed, were fraudulent. This statute created the offence of 'acting as a spiritualistic medium or using telepathy, clairvoyance or other fraudulent powers with intent to deceive or when so acting using any fraudulent device when it is proved that the person so acted for reward'. The Act, however, did not forbid this kind of thing for entertainment purposes, but, surprisingly, it did repeal the Witchcraft Act of 1735! It is quite remarkable that in 1951 witches could still be prosecuted in England and Wales.

In country areas, however, there were people who could produce some kind of healing potion from plants found in the wild, there were those who could forecast the weather with bits of seaweed or aching limbs, those who believed they could cure the ailments of others by the laying on of hands, those who could forecast the near future, and others with similar genuine or supposed extra-sensory skills.

None of these could be described as either witches or mediums and I never came across any who sought to make money from their talents or beliefs.

Around the 1950s and 1960s, however, the Sunday newspapers would often feature the activities of spiritualists and mediums, with sneaked photographs of them at work in seances or, while in a trance, producing ectoplasm, which looked rather like a huge wodge of white candy floss. Many of these were later proved fraudulent. In exposing frauds in this way, the newspapers did some good work, for the mediums were little more than clever illusionists and conjurors out to make a few pounds from vulnerable and gullible people. It was the activities of such tricksters which had led to the passing of the Fraudulent Mediums Act.

In spite of the tricksters there are people who can apparently 'see' future events and perform other amazing feats which defy logical explanation. My great aunt, for example, regularly dreamed the winners of horse races before the races were run. There are people who 'see' aircraft crashes and other disasters before they happen and others with an uncanny knack of accurately forecasting events. It is probably people with such highly developed senses who see ghosts — and there was such a character in Rannockdale. But, when looking at him or talking to him, he was the last person one would have expected to have any kind of extra-sensory skills. He was a farm labourer in his sixties, a man with little or no education and he lived with his wife in a tied house at High Rock Farm in the upper reaches of Rannockdale. He was called Jared Longstaff and he had worked at High Rock since leaving school at the age of fourteen.

I don't think he had ever been out of the dale except for the occasional trip to Stokesley Show and one day out at Scarborough — which he had not enjoyed due to the crowds and traffic. Whenever I paid an official visit to High Rock, I would see Jared around the premises, a thick-set man always dressed in overalls complete with a pale-blue flat cap and black boots. With warm brown eyes, he had a round and jolly face reddened by the weather of the high moorland, and a wonderful gingery moustache which extended beyond his cheeks. I think his hair had been ginger too, but I never saw him without his cap and the hair which did show beneath it was now turning grey. His hands were thick, large and powerful, and yet he had a wonderful delicacy and tenderness when dealing with small animals, like lambs, calves and tiny chicks. He did everything on the farm — milking, mucking out the cowhouse, feeding the geese and hens, collecting eggs, repairing dry stone walls, clearing ditches, haymaking, riddling potatoes and the host of other tasks that need to be done to keep a farm running efficiently every day of the year. Whatever had to be done, Jared was capable of doing it. He was a real asset to the farmer, Bill Norton, whose family had owned this farm for more than 200 years. Jared never seemed to want a day off or to leave his home. So far as I know, he had never been away on holiday, he had never owned a car and had little idea of life beyond the spectacular scenery of the farm where he had spent his entire life. His wife would walk to the lane end to catch a bus into Ashfordly for her bits of shopping, but that seemed the extent of her social life too. They were a very contented couple, I thought, although they had never produced any children.

Some might have seen them in a different light, perhaps feeling they lacked initiative and drive, or that they had no sense of adventure, but not once did I hear either of them complain about their lifestyle.

But Jared had an amazing talent. I do not know how or when he realised his skills, but I became aware of it one Sunday afternoon when I popped into Ashfordly Police

Station. Alf Ventress was performing a spell of office duty and he was behind the counter when a lady entered.

'Hello, Mrs Britten, what brings you here?' Alf greeted her.

As I was making entries in the 'Visits to Licensed Premises' register I heard her say, 'Ah, Mr Ventress. I'm glad I've caught you. I'm not sure whether you are the right person to talk to, but I have lost my watch.'

'Lost? Or do you think it's been stolen?' Alf put to her.

'Oh, I'm sure it's not been stolen. It was on my wrist this morning — I put it on when I got up — and then when I wanted to check the time over lunch in the Black Swan, I noticed it was missing. I've been in town since half past ten and could have lost it somewhere here. I wondered if it had been handed in.'

'Well, we've not received any reports so far, and I've been in the office all day,' he said. 'But I suppose there is time. I'll make a note and if it is found, we'll contact you. Perhaps it would be a good idea to revisit the places you've been to, and ask around? Like the Black Swan and the shops.'

'I've done that, Mr Ventress. It could still be at home, of course; it might have slipped from my wrist before I set off. I'll have a good look around when I get back.'

'You'll let us know if it does turn up?'

'I will. I do hope I find it, Mr Ventress, it was a wedding present, from my husband.' And she then gave a good clear description of the missing watch which Alf recorded in the Lost Property Register.

'If it's of deep sentimental value,' he smiled, after he had completed his entry, 'you could always have a chat with Jared Longstaff. He's done wonders for others.'

'I have heard about him,' she smiled. 'People speak highly of his skills. I'll have a look around the house when I get back and if I don't come across it, I might drive up to Rannockdale and see Jared.'

Having completed the matter, Mrs Britten left and so I took the opportunity to quiz Alf about Jared — whom I already knew.

'What was that about seeing Jared Longstaff?' I asked.

'Oh, he's supposed to be good at finding things,' Alf said. 'You know how some folks visit fortune tellers and the like, wanting advice about their future, well, when folks lose things hereabouts, sentimental things, as a rule, they go and see Jared. They have to see him in person, he likes to touch the place the object vanished from, like a wrist in this case or an ear for an ear-ring, or a finger if a ring has gone, that sort of thing, and then he tells the loser where to look. Most times, he's right. He's not a hundred per cent reliable, possibly because somebody else has already found the lost object and nicked it.'

'It'll be luck, won't it?' I could not understand this. 'How can he locate things when the owners can't?'

'Search me!' said Alf. 'I don't think Jared knows how he does it. Just like Catholics pray to St Anthony of Padua if they want to find lost belongings, so the folks hereabouts rely on Jared and make pilgrimages to High Rock Farm.'

'Well, I've never heard about it, and Jared's never said anything whenever I've chatted to him.'

'He doesn't talk about it; he doesn't know how he does it. All he knows is that if somebody takes the trouble to go and see him, he can usually point to the place where the property can be found. It does seem as if it has to be something very personal, though, something of sentimental value, not necessarily something worth a lot of money.'

Alf then told me of instances within his personal knowledge where Jared had been successful — a man had lost a valuable pocket watch which had belonged to his grandfather, and Jared told him to look under a sideboard at home. The watch chain had broken, and it had rolled along the carpet to come to rest behind the leg of the sideboard, well out of sight. A woman had mislaid a photograph of her mother — Jared told her to look in the loft. The woman had been clearing out some cupboards and had inadvertently picked up the photograph with some old cloths she'd used to cover those belongings stored in the loft. A woman had lost a diamond ear-ring somewhere in the house and in spite of a thorough search, had failed to find it; Jared told her to look in the compost bin! She'd been peeling potatoes when the ear-ring had slipped from her pierced ear to fall among the peelings.

These were just a few of the examples quoted by Alf Ventress, and the outcome was that Alf often recommended upset losers to contact Jared if all else failed. I must admit that a lot of the success in the examples given was due to little more than common sense. By retracing one's steps and working out just where one had been at the material time, it was often possible to recover a lost object.

It would be five or six days later when I was chatting to Alf and he said, 'Oh, Nick, you remember that Mrs Britten? She'd lost her watch.'

'Right,' I acknowledged. 'And you told her to contact Jared Longstaff.'

'Yes, well, she's found it. She rang to say thank you. She went to see Jared, he held her wrist and told her to look in the garage. She did — and she found it. It had fallen from her wrist as she was getting into the car and she'd unknowingly kicked it; it had gone under the workbench and was lying among a lot of leaves which had blown in during the autumn. You'd never have seen it unless you'd removed all the leaves, which she did because Jared suggested it.'

'But surely, Alf, that's common sense again. You search all the places you've been to at the material time . . .'

'But she'd already searched the garage once, Nick, she did that when she left here, and she didn't see it. It required Jared to convince her it could be there.'

'Well, I don't see it was extraordinary — it's down to common sense in thoroughly searching all the likely places.'

'Well, I'd back Jared any time!' said Alf. 'All I can say is that he's come up trumps time and time again and made a lot of folks very happy.'

I must admit I forgot about Jared and his alleged skills until a tragedy occurred near Crampton. One Sunday afternoon, two small boys, neighbours and friends, were playing on the riverbank about half a mile to the south of Crampton, at a place called Otters Pool. There, the river sweeps around a wide bend as it changes direction to flow to the left, and at that point the powerful and fast-flowing current has worn away much of the right-hand bank; a deep and rather sinister pool has been formed there, albeit with water continually flowing slowly through it while the mainstream flows past on the left. One of the boys, Paul Bailey, aged seven, had crawled along the dead branch of a tree which overhung the pool; the branch had cracked, and he had tumbled into the deep water. Unable to swim, he'd struggled and spluttered until he'd finally disappeared under the surface as his little friend, Sammy Woodford, had run for help.

Within minutes, many people including the respective families and myself were at the scene, but there was no sign of Paul, other than the broken branch which was floating in the shallows of Otters Pool. I organized a speedy search of the riverbanks downstream and then, fearing the lad had drowned, radioed for assistance in the form of our Underwater Search Unit. It was estimated it would take an hour for the officers to arrive, and in the meantime two powerful swimmers, male friends of the families, dived into Otters Pool, which was some twelve feet deep in places, but in spite of their prolonged search, they found no sign of the boy. When the USU arrived, their two officers conducted a thorough and painstaking search of the pool and both banks of the river downstream but found nothing.

From them, we learned that the underwater stretches of the river at that point consisted of many small caves, scooped out with the actions of the flow over the centuries, and there were some very deep fissures on the river-bed too, most of them too narrow to admit the underwater search officers. It was feared that Paul's body might have become lodged in one of those, completely beyond recovery. Guided by the underwater experts, we completed a long and arduous search of the river both on the surface and beneath, extending it to well over a mile downstream, but we found no sign of the missing

Paul. Our search extended to the riverbanks, in the vain hope he might have struggled ashore, but we found nothing. That he was dead was beyond doubt, a sad reality which his parents had difficulty in accepting without the evidence of his body, and so what began as a search to hopefully save his life now became a matter of recovering his mortal remains.

The onset of darkness meant that the search had to be abandoned, by which time Sergeant Craddock, Alf Ventress, Phil Bellamy and some officers from Brantsford had arrived, along with a team of police dogs and two more underwater search experts. But in spite of the anguished pleas from Paul's parents, we had to abandon the search until first light the following morning. It was agreed that the entire search team would reassemble at six o'clock on the banks beside Otters Pool.

Unknown to me or any of the other officers, Paul's father, Colin Bailey, had been persuaded by his wife, Betty, to go and see Jared Longstaff. From her mother, she'd heard about his supposed ability to rediscover lost, sentimental valuables and in her deep emotional state, had decided to seek his help. After all, she had reasoned, could anything have more sentimental value than a missing child? We knew nothing of this until the following morning. While our teams began to assemble near Otters Pool and as Sergeant Craddock began to assemble everyone and allocate tasks, it was Alf Ventress who noticed that Mrs Bailey was carrying half a bread loaf. He drew my attention to it.

'She's been to see old Jared,' was all he said, *sotto voce*.

'Jared?' For the moment, the significance of this escaped me and then I realised what he meant. 'So what's she going to do with the loaf?'

As Mrs Bailey made her way towards the edge of the water, to a safe point some twenty yards upstream from the damaged tree, Sergeant Craddock noticed her.

'Ah, Mrs Bailey, you are putting some kind of tribute on the water, are you? We can delay our search for a few moments, that's if you wish to say prayers or something . . . do you wish to float a candle or flowers down river? Is that it?'

'Oh, no.' She shook her tearful head. 'This is to help you to find him, I've been to see Jared.'

'Jared?' he puzzled.

'I'll explain later, Sergeant,' Alf stepped in with a timely interruption. 'I suggest we let Mrs Bailey do as she wishes.'

I had no idea what she was about to do, but we made no attempt to dissuade her for we all recognised her actions as a cry of desperation. From her handbag she took a small phial of grey liquid and poured it into the scooped-out centre of the half-loaf, then placed the bread upon the river and it floated downstream.

It moved quite rapidly with the fast flow and it passed directly beneath the fatal branch, but instead of moving into the placid pool, it maintained its course with the mainstream and moved very quickly away from the extremities of the pool.

'Follow it,' she cried. 'Watch where it comes to rest.'

For a moment, there was silence, and then Craddock said, 'Do as she says!'

Ventress said to me, 'It's an old belief, Nick; she's put mercury into the hollowed bread, from a broken thermometer or two I'd guess, and it's thought that wherever the bread comes to rest, the body will be beneath it. It's a very old notion, but used in modern times . . . I remember a case in 1953, on the Bridgewater Canal in Cheshire . . .'

'All right, PC Ventress, we get the message,' said Craddock. 'Now, let's see where this goes. Come along, all of you!'

And so it was that the gathering of police officers, including two clad in the diving suits of the Underwater Search Unit and a handful of volunteers from the village, began to hurry along the right-hand bank, skirting the pool and struggling through thick vegetation and riverside trees as they strove to keep the bobbing loaf of bread in sight. Fortunately, its white colour meant it was highly visible during its journey, but because it was being carried by the mainstream current, it was moving very rapidly. It made us realise just how fast and strong were the currents of water, but the surface movements gave no clue as to what was happening beneath. The loaf swirled around the left-hand bend, now leaving Otters Pool behind as it bobbed and wove into the rougher area.

In places, the water was quite shallow as it coursed over a bed of rocks and boulders, but those areas concealed many very deep parts; there were what amounted to miniature white-water rapids, with swirling white-foamed waves offset with surprisingly calm pools. It was clear that the river rushed along a course filled alternatively with deep crevices beneath and rocky surfaces above. In our headlong gallop, we crashed through the undergrowth for almost a mile, still with the bobbing loaf in view and then it came to rest.

It bounced and rocked down a series of white-water rapids and came to rest in one of the calm pools, this time beneath an overhanging cliff of moorland granite. The pool was on our side of the river, the right-hand side when heading downstream, which meant our teams did not have to cross the water. The overhanging rock appeared to conceal a deep underwater cavern. Now, the bread appeared to have completed its journey.

The underwater search officers looked at Sergeant Craddock for guidance, he looked at Ventress, sensing he knew more about this sort of thing than the rest of us, and Ventress, looking grim, caught the eye of Mrs Bailey and said, 'I suggest we make a start by searching that pool, Sergeant.'

Craddock said, 'Well, I must admit it is much further downstream than I would have expected but it does make a good starting point. If we find nothing here, we can work our way upstream to Otters Pool. Right, gentlemen,' he now addressed the underwater team. 'It all depends on you.'

They found Paul under that rock.

His poor little body showed signs of battering and bruising as the powerful currents had carried him to this final resting place, and his parents were allowed a few moments with his body before it was transported away for the awful but necessary procedures which accompany such sudden deaths.

But they did have a body, they did have a result and they could mourn him. That was very important.

It was later in Ashfordly Police Station as I was finalising my 'Sudden Death' report that Sergeant Craddock said, 'PC Rhea, I don't think we need make reference to the bread loaf and mercury, need we? I mean, we would have searched that pool in due course, and we cannot give credence to such superstitious practices, can we?'

'Oh, I don't know,' chipped in Alf Ventress. 'I mean, Sergeant, that loaf did come to rest where the body was found . . . now, you might put that down to coincidence, but the lad's mother believed it. And for her it worked.'

'Worked? It was a coincidence, PC Ventress! Nothing more! How can you say it worked?'

But at Sergeant Craddock's insistence, I did not refer to the bread loaf and mercury in my official report, nor was any reference made to the custom at the coroner's inquest. We simply said that Paul Bailey's body had been found as the result of a search by the Underwater Search Unit and so the part played by the bread does not feature in any formal account.

Later, when I called at High Rock Farm for my quarterly check of the stock register, Jared spotted me. 'They found that lad, then?' was all he said.

'Yes, they did. Thanks, Jared,' I smiled.

CHAPTER 8

It could be argued that the 1960s witnessed the first real surge in the practice of day-tripping by car. Even for a few years after the end of World War II, many working-class people could not afford holidays, but if they managed to save the necessary funds, they went to the seaside and usually travelled by coach or train because they did not own a car. They stayed in boarding-houses or holiday camps and enjoyed amusement arcades, fruit machines, bingo halls, talent contests, pubs and clubs, fish-and-chip shops and playing cricket or football (or even sunbathing), on the glorious sandy beaches of the Yorkshire resorts. The professional classes, on the other hand, with their cars, could afford more expensive breaks and they would either spend time overseas or take leisurely holidays in British hotels from where they went fishing for salmon, walking in the hills or spending their time enjoying informative and refined pursuits such as visiting museums and art galleries. Such people did not laze around on the beach all day, nor did they indulge in kiss-me-quick hats, candy floss, winkle-eating and knobbly-knees contests as part of their holiday fun.

But higher incomes for everyone, along with shorter working hours and easier ownership of motor vehicles changed the leisure industry. The so-called ordinary people were able to afford a car, and this allowed greater access to beauty spots and holiday areas, not only on the coast but also inland in the moors and dales. In enjoying these trips, however, many were still cautious with their cash and opted for shorter breaks rather than a whole week. They went for the day's outing and took a picnic.

Although some discovered it was cheap to fly to continental resorts, a very broad spectrum of townspeople began to explore the British countryside in a way they had never previously done. Instead of joining a coach party for a mystery tour or an organized outing to a stately home or zoo, they made their own decisions and travelled in family cars. Outings were more affordable and could therefore be more frequent, especially if one took one's own food. Another bonus was that one could return home the same day and have enough time to pop to the pub or club for a pint or two. As a consequence, day trips became very popular and there is little doubt they allowed many who would not otherwise see the countryside to gain access to some of our lovelier places.

One unexpected outcome of this change was that people from the south of England began to realise the north was very attractive in spite of valiant efforts by northerners to deter them by conveying the impression it was all pit heaps, whippets and working-men's clubs. Thanks to the motor car, our best-kept northern secret was revealed — millions discovered that North Yorkshire is an incredibly beautiful place.

In addition to the day-trippers and tourists, however, workmen began to expand their activities into the countryside. Town-bred artisans began to win contracts to work in rural places because they could travel from home and return within the same day having completed the task in question. Although some urban workmen caused problems, such as the notorious Leeds Gangs (confidence tricksters who persuaded householders to part with cash for botched and needless repairs to walls and roofs), others did a very good and professional job.

It could be said they won their contracts at the expense of their rustic counterparts, but rural dwellers also found it quite easy to commute to work in the towns. For some, because town domestic rates were expensive, it made economic sense to live in a country cottage with a low rateable value and commute to town. Many felt this was better than living permanently in a town or suburban environment; they preferred the quality of life in the countryside and were quite happy to pay for the privilege through the cost of their car and the additional time required to get to work. That logic prevails today, with some commuters travelling enormous distances so they can enjoy peaceful rural weekends.

The pride in owning one's own mode of transport was another factor and this meant few people had to depend on the unreliable and at times dirty trains and bus services. The private car provided a wonderful sense of freedom and joy.

However, not every townie had the breadth of knowledge required for living and working in the countryside. For some, it was an alien environment. I had a wonderful example with a small firm of painters and decorators from Stockton-on-Tees who managed to win a contract for some work on my beat. Their task was to paint a water-tower on Craydale Estate. Viscount Craydale was the local landowner and because his estate was both extensive and hilly, there was a water-tower on its western boundary. It was used to gather rain which could then be used for watering his cattle or irrigating the land which lay some distance from the nearest mains supply.

It reminded me of those watch-towers used by Nazi prisoner-of-war camps for it was a large oblong water tank set high upon an iron framework which looked like a modern electricity pylon. A long ladder was bolted to one side to provide access to the tank for maintenance purposes, and although the water-tower was very useful, it was somewhat unsightly. Its unhappy appearance was aggravated by the rigours of the North Yorkshire climate which meant it became rusty from time to time; it was in need of constant care and attention, and new coats of paint. Many estates had similar towers. In addition to the tank, the iron framework supporting this one had developed a rather urgent need for renovation.

Viscount Craydale's estate manager had placed an advertisement in the local paper seeking competent work-men to undertake that commission, and a response had come from a small firm calling themselves Distinctive Decorators. Their estimate was by far the most reasonable, even though it entailed a daily trip from Stockton, and so the estate had issued the necessary order.

I learned of this one bright summer morning when I was performing an early patrol. It was a brilliant sunny day. A small green van eased to a halt at the telephone kiosk at which I was standing; I was making a point — if the office wanted to contact me, they could ring on the public tele-phone because I would be there at a certain time, 8 a.m. on that particular morning. The van contained two men in white, paint-spattered overalls and a lot of material associated with the decoration trade — tins of paint, stripper, ladders, wallpaper and so on.

The sides of the van bore the legend *Distinctive Decorators* with a Stockton-on-Tees address and telephone number. Even as this first van eased to a halt at my side, a second one, identical to the first, also came to a halt. It contained more painting materials and another two men in white overalls.

'Excuse me, mate,' said the passenger in the first vehi-cle, using the unattractive and featureless Teesside accent. 'Where can I find Craydale Estate?'

I gave him directions, suggesting he make for the estate office and he understood. 'Thanks, mate. See you,' and off went both vans.

I thought no more of that little incident until eight o'clock that same evening when I received a call from PC Rogers, the duty constable at Eltering Police Station.

'Nick, I've had a call from Stockton Police,' he said. 'Sorry to bother you after your tour of duty, but we've a

141

missing person enquiry, well, four missing persons to be precise. On your patch. The company secretary has called us.'

'Crumbs!' I expounded. 'So what's the story?'

'Not very dramatic,' he said. 'More peculiar than dramatic. Four painters came over to our part of the world this morning, from Stockton; they've got a couple of vans with the name on the side — Distinctive Decorators. They were commissioned to paint the water-tower on Craydale Estate.'

'I met them,' I said. 'Early this morning. I directed them to Craydale.'

'Right, that means they got there. Well, according to this lady, who is the wife of one of them, they should have finished work at four-thirty, and been back in Stockton by six o'clock at the latest. They've not returned, Nick, and the lady has had no word from them. We've had no reported accidents or hospital casualty admissions. The secretary's grown a little worried. If they're going to be late they always let her know, but she's heard nothing and time's getting on. She rang Craydale Estate, but the office is closed, and she got no reply. Inspector Breckon wonders if you would mind driving over to Craydale, to see if you can find out what's happened to them? They drove across the moors in two vans, so it's odd if they've both had problems.'

'I'll go,' I said. 'I'll call when I have some news.'

'Thanks,' and Rogers rang off.

Calls of this kind, out of normal working hours, were not unusual in the daily routine of a rural constable, and I would adjust my duty time on some future occasion; the fate of those painters was more important than my leisure time. Within minutes, I was speeding to Craydale in my van, wondering what could have happened to them. Had they suffered some kind of accident in that remote corner of the estate? There were some old pit shafts on the moors, and another problem was the presence, in some areas, of unexploded bombs, relics of World War II. An accident might befall a single person out alone on the moors, but four men in two vans? It seemed unlikely.

When I arrived in Craydale village, the gates to the estate were open as they often were, but I checked the estate office and found it closed. I considered a visit to the home of Ian Humble, the estate manager, but because I knew the location of the water-tower, I decided to make a direct approach. After all, they might still be working, anxious to complete some task before tomorrow, albeit without the means of contacting their office, but if the painters had got into difficulties, time was vital.

On that light, warm summer evening, therefore, I drove through the undulating landscape of Craydale Estate and eventually saw the distinctive outline of the water-tower in the distance. As I drew closer, I could see that four men were still up aloft, their figures silhouetted against the sky as they stood on the platforms which marked each level. There were two men on each of the two stages and when they noticed my van, they all waved vigorously and began to shout.

I drove closer and saw their vans parked below the tower, but also on the ground below was a herd of Shorthorn cows, about fifty in all. Some were lying on the ground, and some were on their feet, munching at the grass around the tower. I parked and climbed out of my van, an action which caused the cows to move forward to inspect me and my van, then I made my way through the herd. Cows are the most inquisitive of animals — if you sit in a field which contains cows and decide to have a picnic, they will come towards you and stand in a large semi-circle looking at you. But that's all they will do, although a brave animal might reach out its nose to sniff at you or your food. But if you stretch out a hand to pat it, it will withdraw nervously. Cows will rarely attack or harass anyone, although a protective mother cow with a calf might not be quite so friendly. But none of these had calves. It was a dairy herd which had recently been milked, then turned out into this meadow.

But these men didn't seem to understand that.

I heard one of them shout down to me, 'Thank God you've come, I thought we was going to up here all bloody night . . . let us get down, Constable, shift them bulls.'

'What bulls?' I called back, as I continued through the assembled cows towards the base of the tower.

'Them bloody bulls, look at them horns . . . They all came and surrounded us, just as we was going to pack up.'

'And you've been stuck up there ever since?' I laughed.

'We have, since half four. It's not funny, Constable, we're not used to bulls, you know. God knows where they all came from, but they're lying in wait to attack us the minute we get down and we haven't any red capes. We're not bull-fighters. Call us cowards if you like, but we're not coming down till they've all gone.'

'These are not bulls!' I shouted to them. 'They're cows. A dairy herd.'

'They've all got horns,' shouted their spokesman. 'Look at them horns . . .'

'Some cows do have horns, but it doesn't mean they're bulls,' I laughed. 'Look, I'm walking through them with no trouble, they're getting up and moving away.'

I demonstrated that by walking through the gathered cows; some rose to their feet and moved away while others merely shifted aside a little, but always observing my progress with their typical curiosity. Eventually I was standing beneath the water-tower at the foot of the access ladder.

'Right,' I said. 'Your office has been on the phone. They're wondering what's happened . . . that's why I am here. To see if you need help.'

'You mean those animals are harmless?' called one of them.

'Of course they are, they're milk cows. They'd have been taken in for milking and then turned out on this patch of grassland. When they spotted you and your vans, they'd want to come and have a look, like children do. They're not ganging up to attack you.'

The men said nothing. They could see that I had walked through the herd without any kind of problem, and I am sure they were now debating whether these animals were male or female. Perhaps the distinction was not easy to make from aloft, especially because they had horns, but after some banter and further chat, one of them said, 'Right, Constable, you stay there — don't let those bulls come any closer . . . and I'll come down.'

With what must have been a considerable act of bravery, the first painter decided he would show the others that he was not afraid of a bunch of animals, whatever sex they were, and soon he was descending the ladder. The cows moved away at his descent and this gave him some confidence — eventually, he was standing on the ground below the tower with the cows all on their feet looking at him. He lowered himself to a stooping position and shouted 'Boo', at which the cows all retreated, puzzled.

'They're as nervous as bloody kittens,' he shouted. 'Come on down, you cowards.'

It took but a few minutes for all four to reach safety at ground level as the cows watched their descent. Then one of them came to me.

'Look,' he said, as the cows surrounded him. 'This makes us look daft, eh? You won't tell anybody, will you? That they were cows?'

'I'll radio my sub-division to say you have been traced and that you are fit and well, and on your way home. What you tell them at home is up to you.'

'We could say we was trapped by a herd of rampaging bulls breathing fire and smoke—'

'Or we could say we had to work overtime,' suggested one of them.

'Aye, that might be best,' they said, getting into their vans and driving away.

I radioed Eltering Police Station and said, 'Rhea speaking. Painters found safe and well, no problems. They needed to work overtime to finish a section of the remote tower they were working on and couldn't contact their office.'

'Really?' said PC Rogers. 'I'll bet they'd gone to the pub for a pint or two before going home. That well-used excuse of working late sounds a load of bull to me.'

'It's got them off the horns of a dilemma,' I returned.

* * *

Another instance of a townsperson having problems in the countryside came to light one Sunday afternoon when I received a call from Alf Ventress. At the time, he was staffing Ashfordly Control Room.

'Ah, Nick,' he said. 'A motorist has rung from a kiosk in Rannockdale, he says there's a problem on Dale Head Bank, a blockage, a broken-down vehicle he thinks. There's quite a queue of traffic on both sides of the blockage. Holiday traffic, he reckons. Are you near enough to check it out before we call out a breakdown truck? It's Sunday and they charge double-time on Sundays. We need to be sure what we're doing.'

'Will co. I'm five minutes away,' I replied. 'I'll give you an update as soon as possible.'

I knew Dale Head Bank. It led down a steep and picturesque moorland slope from the lofty main road. Running between high dry, stone walls, it was a very narrow and rather twisting lane with a long climb up a gradient of 1-in-3 (33 per cent). The hill had not been surfaced with tarmac until some years after the end of the war. Even in the 1950s, it had been a mud track with lots of protruding rocks and stones, and capable of use only by a horse and cart, or perhaps a tractor and trailer. No other motor vehicle, except perhaps a scrambles motor bike, would or could have used it. But, as traffic increased, the county council decided to create new foundations for the road and then surface it to provide greater access to the dale. From that time, it became very popular with tourists due to the challenge it presented and for the magnificent views from the summit.

In massed start cycle races, it was also used as a 'prime' (pronounced *preem,* as in the Tour de France); there was a special prize for the cyclist who was first to cross the line at the summit. And he deserved every penny! Not surprisingly, a range of vehicles was forbidden to use the bank which included coaches, lorries, articulated vehicles and, of course, caravans. In our experience, day-trippers and tourists should have been forbidden too, because few seemed able to cope with the gradient.

As a local farmer once said to me, 'There's nowt wrong wi t'cars, it's them daft folks who can't drive 'em properly.'

My call to Dale Head Bank on this occasion was a perfect example of the proof of that farmer's statement and it reminded me of the event involving the caravan on Sutton Bank (mentioned earlier in this collection of tales). But in this case, there was an additional element.

As I drove into the village I could see the stationary queue of traffic as it formed a crocodile of cars and small vans on the hill at the far side of the dale. Likewise, the down-coming traffic was also queueing. The vehicles at the front of each queue were unable to turn around due to the narrowness of the carriageway. Furthermore, they could not reverse because additional cars had arrived to block the lane behind them. I realised that drivers of the late arriving vehicles, both on the up and down routes, would not be able to see the cause of the problem, but from my elevated approach at the opposite side of the dale I could see a pale, tan-coloured motor car stationary between those vehicles trying to ascend the hill and those endeavouring to descend. It was partially across the road on a bend and was very effectively blocking both very narrow lanes. From the distance, it looked like a medium-sized family saloon. I parked on the forecourt of the Methodist chapel at the foot of Dale Head Bank and walked up the hill, drivers opening their doors to ask, 'What's the problem, Officer?' 'Is there a crash?' 'Can you get us moving, I'm supposed to be in Scarborough in ten minutes?' 'We've been stuck here for ages, why doesn't somebody do something?'

After a steep climb which quickly had me panting for breath, I reached the cause of the problem. As I had anticipated, it was a family saloon, a Hillman Minx, but it contained only one person. He was a man in his late forties, balding with dark hair, and with a round, pale face. He was dressed in blue slacks and a neat light-blue shirt, and when he realised I was approaching, he climbed out of his car and stood beside it, with the driver's door open.

'Cor blimey, mate—' he was a Cockney by the sound of his voice — 'Am I glad to see you!'

'What's the problem?' I asked.

'Given up the ghost, she 'as. Conked out on me. Won't go another inch . . . ain't never seen an 'ill like this before! Talk abaht an 'ouse-ender . . .'

'So what's broken? Do I need a breakdown truck, and can it be towed?'

'She shudders and conks aht whenever I try to move 'er, so I fort it best not to damage 'er; she's an 'ire car, mate. Got 'er for the week, I 'ave. Don't want to cause damage to 'er innards, do I? Look, we need to git 'er shifted, all them geezers aht there are getting restless . . . natives, eh? Getting restless . . .' And he laughed at his own version of a joke. ''Ere, tell you what, you get in and see, then you can tell the breakdown geezers. 'E'll want to know whether to tow me in or fetch a low-loader, although Gawd knows 'ow they'll get a lorry up 'ere, mate . . . I ain't never seen 'ills like this, I ain't. Beats Crystal Palace any day, it does.'

'Didn't any of the other motorists offer help?'

'Sure they did, mate, but I said no way, no way was I goin' to let them git their 'ands on this motor, not in the state it's in. Then a geezer said 'e'd ring for the boys in blue and get 'elp.'

'Right.' I didn't get in but said, 'Show me what it does.'

He clambered back into the driving seat and then I noticed the rear seat was packed with luggage.

'On me own, I am,' he said noticing my glance at his luggage. 'Tourin'. Got a bootful of garden things wot I've bought up 'ere, stone troughs an' gnomes an' things . . . for the garden back in the Smoke.'

'Right, well, there's quite a heavy load, but show me the problem.'

'Well.' He started the engine and it ticked over nicely with no sign of a problem, and then, somewhat nervously, he put the car into gear, engaged the clutch and released the handbrake. It snatched and shuddered violently, then, with a shudder, the engine cut out.

'There you are, mate. Somefing's gorn underneaf, drive shaft eh?'

'No,' I said. 'You're trying to make a hill start in second gear. There's no wonder it won't move!'

'What d'yer mean, second gear? This thing has three gears and I'm using first.'

'No, it's got four gears and you're using second,' I said. 'I know lots of folks set off in second, on the flat, but in these parts where there are real hills, you need bottom gear, it's there for a purpose. Now, push the stick forward, as if for third, but further across to your left.'

'You're joking, mate?' His face began to redden with some embarrassment.

'Try it,' I said.

He obeyed and suddenly found the gear lever sliding smoothly into the gear he did not know existed. He looked at me, sheepishly, and I said, 'Now, go! keep it in bottom gear all the way to the top.'

And the car moved forward with ease and I waved at him not to stop until he reached the summit. He crawled up the hill in first gear and I saw him vanish over the summit; immediately, the other cars began to move, and one or two drivers shouted to the effect of, 'What's the secret, Constable? Magic repairs?'

'No,' I smiled. 'Just a matter of gear selection . . . right gear for the right circumstances.'

'Townie, is he?' chuckled one driver.

'Southerner,' I said. 'Cockney by the sound of him.'

'They don't have hills in London, do they? Not proper ones.'

There was a good deal of banter as I walked to the summit and there I found he had pulled into the side of the road where there was ample space to park. He was standing at the side of his car now, blushing.

'I don't know what to say,' he flushed. 'I must look a real twit, musn't I?'

'You're not the first,' I said. 'Loads of motorists never use bottom gear and forget all about it. Anyway, the problem's over. No breakdown truck needed. Enjoy the rest of the holiday. So where are you going now?'

'Scarborough tonight, seeing my sister, then home to London first thing tomorrow.'

'Back to work on Monday?'

'Worse luck!'

'So what do you do in London?' I asked.

'I'd better not say, or I'll never live this dahn . . .'

'I can keep a secret,' I smiled.

He paused and then said, 'Well, sod it, I'm a taxi driver . . . London cabs an' that.'

* * *

Another problem with townie tourists caused a headache for a farmer called Frank Hopcroft of Elm House Farm, Aidensfield. He owned a large spread on the slopes of the moor above Aidensfield and specialised in growing cereals as well as running a noted dairy herd of the distinctive black and white Friesians. Frank, a Nordic-looking man with a tall, slender figure and long blond hair, was an affable sort of fellow who never seemed to annoy anyone; he made friends with all who came into contact with him. But his legendary friendliness was stretched by trespassing and selfish ramblers who insisted on taking short-cuts across his land.

There was a public footpath around the edge of one of his cornfields; it was clearly marked on Ordnance Survey maps and the beginning of the path, where it entered his land from the main road, was likewise clearly identified with a 'Public Footpath' sign. That portion did not cause problems.

Frank was happy to make sure the stile was always maintained in good condition and that the path around the edge of his land was well maintained and free from obstruction.

Unfortunately, when ramblers were walking from north to south, down the path which descended from the north, they had a clear view of the broad dale below. Nestling in the dale was the attractive village of Elsinby with the Hopbind Inn clearly in evidence from Frank's footpath. It seemed, however, that on occasions the tempting sight of the inn with its noted beers and bar snacks was too much for ramblers. They just had to reach it as soon as possible! They realised that by taking a short cut across Frank's field, making a diagonal trek through the field instead of walking around it, and then using a lane nearby, the trek to the inn could be shortened by almost a mile.

Another way of looking at this was to shorten the walk by, say, twenty minutes, or perhaps even the time it took to sink a welcome pint of bitter. The problem was that most ramblers took to Frank's fields during the spring, summer and autumn months when his new crops were growing and ripening, and they trampled down his precious plants. Furthermore, when newcomers saw the track through the corn, they assumed it was the true footpath and followed it. When Frank tried to redirect them he was faced with a good deal of abuse and so the problem became more serious with each passing month. Eventually, he came to see me about it.

'The worst thing is the abuse,' he said after explaining the problem. 'These people seem to forget my fields are private property — let them use the public footpaths by all means, I don't mind that, but when they trample down my crops and then abuse me when I point out the real route, well, it's enough to make a chap very angry. I don't want to stop them using the proper path, I just want them to stop using my cornfield as a short cut, to respect my work. That's all. So I'm here to seek your advice, Nick.'

'The path is clearly signed?' I asked. 'And kept clear of obstructions? No barbed wire?'

'No, I spend time and money doing that; I want people to enjoy the countryside and learn about it, But I expect them to behave sensibly. So what can I do?'

'The first thing I have to say, Frank, is that civil trespass is not a police matter. Even if I see the people rambling across your cornfield, I have no powers to stop them, or deal with them. And all you can do, in the first instance, is ask them to leave.'

'I know that, and I do try to redirect them to the official path. When I ask them and explain things, most will do so. But some are terrible people, Nick. You'd think I was their enemy or something.'

'If people persistently refuse to leave upon request, you can take out a civil court injunction to ban them in the future, but that takes time and money and, of course, you do not know their names. I suppose you could seek an injunction to prevent all ramblers trespassing, and then erect a notice to warn them about it. If they breach the injunction, it amounts to contempt of court, and that carries severe penalties.'

'That's a bit heavy handed, Nick. But if they cause damage, it makes a difference?'

'Yes, if they deliberately cause damage while trespassing, then we might be able to prosecute them. The police could become involved if that happened. The Malicious Damage Act of 1861 creates the offence of damaging growing crops, and it allows the landowner to arrest anyone found committing the offence. So yes, that is one option. But we need to prove that the damage was malicious.'

'I don't like the idea of arresting folks, it's not my way of doing things, Nick. I could put notices up, I suppose, asking them to avoid my crops, but it seems the determined crowd would ignore them. I could, I suppose, fence in the footpath so that they don't stray from it.'

'Determined rambling vandals would climb over it, Frank, then you'd be faced with repairs to the fence.'

'There must be some simple way to stop them using that field as a short cut,' he said.

'I don't think there is any official way, other than what we've just discussed,' I had to tell him. 'You can use notices, warning signs, that sort of thing. That's about all.'

'I did think of rerouting the path across the field, and leaving that part unsown, but if I interfere with the official route, I'll get into bother, won't I?'

'Probably. Those who defend our footpaths seem to think it is more serious than cruelty to children, or shoplifting . . .'

'I'll think about it,' he said.

'And I'll see if I can find out how others have coped with this problem,' I promised. I did make enquiries but, apart from the measures we had discussed, I found no way to ensure that ramblers did not abuse Frank's privacy. I suggested he make contact with the official responsible for footpaths within the North York Moors National Park, but he was not able to offer any positive advice. It was not even permissible to erect *BEWARE OF THE BULL* signs because there were restrictions on keeping bulls in fields to which the public had access, and the familiar notice trespassers will be prosecuted was meaningless. Trespassers cannot be prosecuted, unless they cause malicious damage. It looked as though Frank would have to tolerate ramblers tramping through his crops even though there was an official footpath nearby. And then Frank had an idea.

Once he had put his idea into fruition, he rang me and suggested that, if I was in the area, I popped in for a coffee and he would reveal his scheme. A couple of days later, I did so. In his spacious farmhouse kitchen, we enjoyed a coffee and buns made by his wife, Ruth, and then we walked to the fields which we'd earlier discussed. As we approached, I saw he had erected several noticeboards, most of which stood alongside his cornfield where it bordered with the official path.

There was another standing close to the start of the unofficial route through this corn. He smiled and led me to that one, saying, 'They're all the same. I had them done by a sign-writer in Ashfordly; he's made a good job of them.'

When I read the notice, it said, with a bold red *warning* sign:

Urtica dioica
Urtica dioica is contiguous to this crop
Endermic contact results in a rash and pain
Please keep to official footpath

'Have you sprayed the field with something?' I asked.

'No,' he smiled. '*Urtica dioica* is the Latin name for the stinging nettle. I'm telling folks they are growing close to this crop and that skin contact can be painful . . . but most folks won't understand. I've tested my sign — within the first couple of hours after I'd erected it, I saw a couple of ramblers look at it and then turn away to use the official path. And I'm not telling a lie, am I? There are plenty of nettles around the edge of that cornfield.'

And so Frank solved his problem. I feel sure many of his rambling townie visitors went home feeling pleased they had not risked a painful attack of *Urtica dioica.*

CHAPTER 9

Sergeant Craddock loved to upbraid us with little pep talks, exhorting us to produce our best efforts to prevent crime, to solve reported crime, to always appear smart and efficient, to be helpful and polite at all times and to remember we were providing a service to the public. He insisted upon tidiness and efficiency in Ashfordly Police Station too, invariably nattering at the office cleaner to keep the surfaces dusted and the floor polished while expressing his disgust at Alf Ventress's trail of cigarette ash and dropped crumbs, or particles of shell from his hard-boiled eggs. He grumbled about young PC Bellamy's unpressed trousers or grubby boots and could not tolerate official papers being left unfiled. He hated a legacy of unsolved crime too, and insisted that we never gave up our investigations, no matter how minor the crime.

'Tidiness is next to Godliness,' he would say from time to time. 'Tidiness of mind and tidiness in behaviour! My mother and father were tidy, and so were my grandparents on both sides, and even my great-grandparents. Tidiness runs in families, gentlemen, like father like son. Criminality is the same; it runs in families. You can see where a father is untrustworthy and idle, then his offspring will be the same . . . remember that during your investigations. You can learn a lot from a family background. And remember the public relies upon us for a great deal of support in times of need. And if they have something stolen from them, even something trivial, they expect us to try and recover it, and to arrest the offender. That is our duty, that is why we are here, gentlemen. Criminals are there to be caught.'

Another of his favourite speeches was, 'If we fail to nip crime in the bud at the smallest of levels, how can we be expected to catch bigger fish? Overlook nothing, gentlemen, a thief is a thief no matter how low the financial value of his greed. Stealing a penny is no different from stealing thousands of pounds. And a child who smashes windows or vandalises parks and gardens will grow up to commit more serious crime unless he is stopped at the very beginning of his criminal career. It is our job to stop criminals developing among the young!'

At other times, he would say, 'Take heed of what you observe about you, gentlemen, in houses you visit, people you encounter, criminals you arrest . . . there are criminal families, you know. If mother goes shoplifting, you can bet the children will steal too . . . it's in the blood, gentlemen. It's all down to breeding — or lack of it!'

His pep talks generally followed the same pattern, but as part of his continuing drive for greater efficiency and tidiness, one of his early tasks was to instruct us to clear the loft at Ashfordly Police Station. At the same time, we had to rid the filing system of all outdated papers — a real spring-clean. From day-to-day files, such as lost dogs, records of official visits to public houses, examination of stock registers, roadside checks of motor vehicles and so forth, everything over ten years old would be removed and discarded. However, Home Office circulars and official orders, instructions and guidance would be maintained, unless they had been officially rescinded, as would details of unsolved major crimes such as murder, rape and robbery. Likewise, files containing details of living criminals, suspected living criminals and other sensitive matters should be retained.

To eliminate doubt, as he put it, if there was any uncertainty in our minds about what or what not to discard, then we should discuss it with Craddock.

The lofts of old police stations tend to emulate the lofts of private houses because they are a convenient dumping ground for all those things, temporarily unwanted, which might have some useful function at some indeterminate future time. For this reason, lots of police station lofts contain a wealth of antiques, from letter scales to office chairs via kettles and inkwells, along with a few truncheons, old helmets, handcuffs and whistles. Posters and memorabilia marking the end of World War I were another treasure, as were those celebrating the Coronation of King George V and the wedding of HRH Princess Elizabeth and the Duke of Edinburgh. The chances are, of course, that such things are never needed again and that their presence in the loft is forgotten. But I think antique dealers could have a wonderful time in police station lofts if only the authorities would permit them.

This ability to assemble junk is especially prevalent in police stations because they do not have permanent residents who can remember what they stored aloft and, likewise, few temporary custodians of the premises wish to spend time clearing out rubbish left by others. Rather, they tend to add to it. The result is that incoming supervisory officers simply have no idea what is stored in the loft above their heads. Because the population of a police station tends to be almost nomadic, always shifting like the sands of time, it means that every new officer-in-charge inherits the cast-off junk, files and paperwork of not just one predecessor, but several. One can understand why they do not wish to spend their valuable time emptying these lofts.

It has to be said that among police officers, there is a tendency to hoard old files, just in case they are required at some future date, but in the chaos of a police-station loft, the chance of actually finding the relevant piece of paper at the time it is required is very remote indeed. In many ways, it is a shame that stuff gets lost in such lofts while a lot of museums, local and national, might be beneficiaries.

In our case, Sergeant Craddock was determined to dispose of tons of out-of-date paperwork. He warned us about the confidential nature of our records and instructed us that the coke-fired central heating boiler be lit and used to burn the clutter. Under no circumstances must any document find its way out of the police station, however old and irrelevant it might appear to be. Dustbins and waste-paper bins would not be used to dispose of old records. He did not want the newspapers or members of the public getting their hands on details of our covert observations of criminals, night-time raids on public houses and sneaky inspections of betting shops, however ancient the records might be. Clearly, he had already undertaken a preliminary exploration of the dark recesses of the loft, in the course of which he had discovered masses of brown paper parcels, all neatly wrapped and dated.

In his opinion, most of them should have been discarded ten years ago, or even twenty years ago, but it seemed that no one had been unduly concerned with such trivia. There were more important things for constabulary attention, such as stray dogs, complaints from residents, low-flying aeroplanes, bikes without lights, late-drinking pubs, idle and disorderly persons and even the occasional crime.

Alf Ventress, the longest-serving constable in Ashfordly and the possessor of an incredible amount of local knowledge, would be second-in-charge of the paper disposal; Craddock himself would be in overall command of the operation. If and when other constables, like myself, were performing duty in Ashfordly, we would be expected to make the necessary time to clean out at least a few files or throw out something from the loft unless of course, we were heavily involved in some other necessary duty. It was to be an on-going commitment with each of us shifting some rubbish every time we came into the office, because there was far too much for it all to be tackled in one operation. The ultimate aim was to have a clean and tidy loft which contained only the most recent of files and the minimum of other discarded objects. Whatever remained in the loft would be clearly labelled and stored in some kind of chronological sequence. And, we had to make room in our office filing cabinets for more relevant and up-to-date material, hence the general cleaning-out of the system.

Craddock said, for example, that prosecutions under the Defence Regulations relating to World War I were hardly worth retaining, neither was an alphabetical list of those Ashfordly residents who had been fined for breaching the blackout restrictions during World War II. Our general opinion was that this had all the hallmarks of a most boring and useless chore and we nicknamed it Operation Lofty, but, as Alf Ventress said, we never knew what gems of local intelligence we might discover. Secrets from several Ashfordly residents were stored in our loft and Alf was sure we would discover them during our clear-out operation.

It was during the preliminary stages of Operation Lofty that some Ashfordly residents began to suspect a sneak thief was active within the town. However, the thief was clever enough to leave doubt in the minds of the victims — some of them did not know whether they had been robbed or not. The technique was very simple — the thief would sneak into a house while the occupant, usually a woman at home during the day, was either upstairs making the beds, or noisily vacuuming in another room, or even next door having a chat and coffee with a neighbour. In these cases, their handbags or purses would be left in the kitchen, often in a prominent position, with the door unlocked.

The thief would sneak in and quickly remove cash from the purse or handbag, but the clever thief did not remove all the money. Inevitably, about a quarter or a third was left behind and, because of this, the victim was not absolutely sure whether or not any money was missing. Some thought they might have spent it without realising, or even lost it in town. There were no signs of a break-in, no damage and nothing else was stolen, although, as we began to receive

159

more complaints about this likely sneak thief, some of the victims mentioned an odd smell. It seemed to linger for a very short time and none could identify it; in the minds of many victims, inevitably women, it indicated someone had been in the kitchen — and that he or she had been there very recently indeed.

My first intimation of these crimes occurred while I was performing a four-hour patrol in Ashfordly one Friday morning. I was pondering the prospect of a half-hour session on Exercise Lofty when a woman approached me in the market place.

'Excuse me, Constable.' She was a small blonde lady, quite plump and mature, and with a broad toothy smile. 'I think I've had some money stolen.'

'You think you have?' I took her up on that point.

'Well, it's difficult to say. I left my purse on the kitchen window ledge while I was upstairs wallpapering. When I came down to make a cup of coffee, I thought there was a funny smell in the kitchen, not a woman's perfume, but something fairly strong; anyway, when I went into my purse to get some money for the insurance man I found there was only two pounds in notes, and about fifteen shillings in cash.'

'So how much did you expect to be there?'

'Well, I can't be completely sure, Constable, but about eight pounds or so. Perhaps ten.'

'So what makes you think it was stolen?'

'I think it was that smell. It made me think somebody had been in the kitchen without me knowing. It didn't last very long, either that or I got used to it, but after thinking it over, I'm sure someone's been in and taken my money.'

'We need to be absolutely sure a crime has been committed before we can officially record it as such,' I said. 'I'll come to your house now, even if the smell has gone, and you can show me the layout of the kitchen.'

'My next door neighbour, Jilly, had a similar experience last week,' she added. 'She didn't report it because she wasn't sure how much money was in her purse.'

'I'll speak to her as well,' I promised.

This first lady's name was Sue Littler. She did not go out to work for she had three children at secondary school. Her husband was a representative for a plastics manufacturer and they lived in a neat semi-detached house on Limetree Grove. To gain entry to the back of the house, through the kitchen, one had to use a concrete pathway which ran behind all the houses. There was a small wooden gate, which did not squeak when I opened it, and this led into a backyard which in turn led into the kitchen. The kitchen window overlooked that backyard and rear footpath — but anyone using the footpath had a clear view of the window sill and whatever was upon it — like a handbag or purse. Having looked at the layout of the kitchen, I realised how easy it was for someone to note that the kitchen was empty and then enter. It was the work of seconds to lift cash from a handbag or purse and then escape.

'So unless you were in the kitchen, you'd not see anyone approaching the back door?'

'No, two of our bedrooms overlook the front and one is at the side; at the back is the bathroom, toilet and staircase window. The lounge and dining room are also at the front, you can't see the back lane from any of those.'

'And the perpetrator could realise you were working upstairs, or he'd hear you if you had a vacuum cleaner working? He — or she — would easily realise you were busy in some other part of the house? He could even tap on the back door without you hearing him — and know the coast was clear.'

'I think so, yes. People do come in without me realising.'

'I must ask the obvious question — did you see anyone suspicious this morning?'

'No, no one, but I didn't leave the house until I came into town. I had some shopping to do, I didn't really intend reporting this because I couldn't be sure I'd lost the money, but when I saw you I thought it sensible to mention it, especially after talking to Jilly, in case you'd heard similar stories.'

'You did the right thing,' I assured her. 'We've not had any other reports, but who's the Jilly you mentioned?'

'Jilly, Mrs Hardey. My neighbour.'

'I'll go and see her, then I'll come back to you.'

Jilly Hartley told a similar tale. Her purse had been lying open on the kitchen table about a week ago, as she had just bought some meat from the butcher who came to the door each week. She'd left her purse open to remind herself to get a birthday card for her mother later in the day. When I checked, I saw it was possible to see the purse on the table from the rear footpath, and she had been upstairs vacuuming the front bedroom just before the theft. When she came downstairs, around eleven o'clock that morning, she'd moved her purse to the mantelshelf, and had then realised it looked emptier than she'd thought. There was some money left in it — about £4 in cash — but she thought some £6 or £7 had gone. She had not reported it to the police because of her uncertainty, but the experience had been revived following her chat to Sue Littler.

'Sue Littler mentioned noticing a funny smell in her kitchen, after the theft,' I put to her. 'Did you?'

'Yes, I did; it was funny, a sweet sort of smell; it didn't last long, but I wondered if it was something I'd been cooking, or something wafting in from outside. I paid no attention to it, not until Sue said she'd experienced it.'

'Any idea what it was? The smell?'

'No, I couldn't identify it. It wasn't a woman's perfume I don't think, or aftershave, and it wasn't minty, not the sort you get when somebody's eating mints or cough sweets. I just have no idea.'

'But you'd recognise it again, if you smelt it?'

'Oh, yes, I think so. It was quite distinctive.'

Having spoken to both women and examined the respective scenes, I felt sure each had been the victim of crime; my next task would be to convince Sergeant Craddock that the women were not mistaken. He'd probably shrink from recording these events as crimes because they'd play havoc with his detection figures if we did not catch the thief and besides, he'd claim the women were mistaken in the actual amount of money they'd had in their purse and handbag. In fact, any evidence of a crime having occurred was very slight indeed and such mistakes were simple to make; it was very easy to lose track of what one had spent, and very easy to lose cash. Before leaving the area, though, I knocked on a few doors and asked householders if they had seen anyone suspicious around the estate at the material times, but everyone shook their heads, and none reported a similar experience.

When I returned to the police station, Alf Ventress was in the loft and one result of his efforts was a large pile of brown paper and string on the office floor. Beside it was a huge pile of foolscap typed paper and old file jackets. I could hear him clumping about and every now and then, a cloud of dust would tumble from the opening to cover the desk and floor. Sergeant Craddock was in his office, avoiding the mess, but when he heard the office door open, he emerged. He was attending to callers while Ventress was working aloft.

'Ah, PC Rhea,' he smiled. 'Another volunteer for loft duties, is it? You might be more capable of throwing things out; PC Ventress seems most reluctant to get rid of any piece of old paper. And Sergeant Blaketon was a hoarder too, you should see the stuff he's hung on to over the years, and then left behind; stuff that's no use to anyone, just cluttering up valuable space.'

'I can't volunteer just now, Sergeant,' I smiled. 'I have received reports of two crimes and thought I had better investigate them.'

'Two crimes? In Ashfordly? We can't have that, PC Rhea! What are they?'

I told him about the suspected sneak thief in the Limetree Grove area and explained what I had done to date and he listened intently.

'You did the right thing, PC Rhea. I trust your judgement in this case, so yes, record them as crimes. There may be more, sneak thieves tend to operate on a long-term basis; if they get away with one or two crimes, they can't resist the temptation to follow with others. It would not surprise me to learn that not all have been reported or will be reported.'

'I did ask around, but no one else experienced a similar occurrence,' I assured him.

'Well done, but time will tell; once one is reported, word reaches other victims and triggers a response. Meanwhile, I shall arrange extra patrols in vulnerable areas, and I think you should knock on a lot more doors, pass the word around in the hope we get other possible victims to come to us. We need to catch this thief; he or she is casting suspicion on lots of people, neighbours and friends of the victims for example, to say nothing of those who call at the houses legitimately, like doctors, nurses, butchers and paper boys. Yes, we must catch this one, PC Rhea. I know there is a tendency in these cases to think no crimes have been committed, that the victims are mistaken, but sneak thieves use that sort of doubt as a cover for their rotten activities. I take these crimes most seriously, so much so that I might even get PC Ventress out of the loft to make enquiries at the other side of town.'

Up aloft, there was a huge thump and a whopping piece of plaster fell from the police-office ceiling and landed behind Craddock to shatter into tiny pieces which spattered under the desks and into the corners.

'Good God, PC Ventress, what on earth is happening up there?' Craddock shouted into the black hole above. 'I think you had better come down before you demolish the entire building! And you had better contact a plasterer, too; we don't want the public to see holes in our office ceilings. Get yourself down here this minute, we need you for more urgent matters.'

'Sorry, Sarge,' said the muffled tones of Alf from the void above. 'I dropped a parcel of unexploded bombs, 1939-1945.'

'You mean you dropped a parcel of papers relating to unexploded bombs, I sincerely hope! You are not saying we have unexploded bombs stored in our loft in addition to all that other stuff, are you?'

'Reports, Sarge, not bangs, not that sort of report. Papers.'

'For heaven's sake, get yourself down here before you cause more damage and frighten us all into evacuating the premises! So long as it is not a bomb, we shall put it in the boiler.'

'Right you are, Sarge, but with all due respect I don't think we should destroy all those files up there, not even the ones about the bombs.'

'Oh, and why not?' asked Craddock.

'Well, if my memory serves me right, all reports of unexploded bombs show their location, and that could imply there are others in the vicinity. That could be very useful if we have to make a search for unexploded bombs on the moors, in the future I mean. Not now. Clusters of them were dropped by the Germans, and not all have been found. There must be dozens more bombs on those moors, Sarge.'

'That may be, PC Ventress, but I have no intention of getting very close to a bomb, unexploded or not.'

'That's what I am saying, Sarge, if we know there they are likely to be, we can keep well clear of them . . .'

'PC Ventress, the war finished in 1945, so I do not think we will get many more, reports.'

'Well, if you say so, Sarge, but I think it is wise to hang on to the file just a little longer.'

'I want you to destroy that file, PC Ventress. If more bombs are found on those moors, you can refer to me and I am sure that whatever happens, it will be done without reference to our ancient filing system.'

And with that, a bundle of files came tumbling from the loft, followed by a cloud of dust and then a very dirty and crumpled constable.

'There we are, Sarge, the job's as good as done. I'll put it in the boiler tomorrow. So what's this urgent job you've got?' Alf brushed his uniform with his hands to send clouds of dust flying to every corner of the office. 'I was quite happy up there, you know, but the trouble is once you get reading an old file, you can't leave it alone. Old files bring back memories, it's like having a good book. You want to know how it all ends, I mean. There's some really fascinating stuff up there, some of those statements dealing with sexual offences, well, they bring a blush to my cheeks and I'm no prude, and that old murder case, 1827 it was, when that magistrate was bumped off for being too familiar with one of the local ladyships . . . I mean, this kind of stuff shouldn't be thrown out, it's important social history.'

'It is not important, PC Ventress, it is trivia, utter rubbish. So forget your dusty heaven for the moment, we have some crimes to occupy our minds. PC Rhea will explain.'

I told Alf what I had learned this morning and he listened carefully, nodding his head and smiling as if I was telling him something he knew already.

'Now isn't that amazing?' he beamed. 'You know what you said, Sarge, about criminal families? Youngsters following the example of their parents? Well, some twenty-five years ago, give or take a few years either way, we had a spate of shoplifting crimes here in Ashfordly. A woman would go into a shop, with a baby in a pushchair — she took the baby and pushchair right in, you could do that in those days — and she would lift small things like tins of soup, baked beans, jars of jam, apples and oranges, or packets of sweets . . . small things she could hide in the pushchair or among the baby's clothes. The shops got wise to her though, and told us, so we set up observations. We got her. Dora Minton. She's still around. In her fifties now, though. She does a bit of tar work and waitressing, but so far as we know, she's kept her nose clean. I think her court appearance frightened her into behaving.'

'All fascinating stuff, I am sure, PC Ventress, but I cannot see what it has to do with our sneak thief?'

'Well, Dora's child was a little girl, Sarge, the one she took on her shoplifting expeditions. She'll be twenty-five now, or thereabouts. Sheila is her name and she's married. Mrs Firthland she now is, and she's got a child of her own, young enough to still be in a pram. You can often see her about town, with the pram. Bonny young lass, very dark hair and dark eyes, gypsy-looking.'

'So you are saying that because her mother was a shop-lifter, Sheila might be our sneak thief?'

'Oh there's more to it than that, Sarge: it's that smell that Nick mentioned.'

'Smell?'

'Yes, when Dora was at the height of her shoplifting powers, she used to get very nervous just before she took things. On a high she was, as they might say now, and she sucked aniseed balls to keep herself calm. Some folks like chewing things at times of stress, like chewing gum and so on. Anyway, that's how the shopkeepers knew she was about the place, they could smell the aniseed — and the moment they smell it, they knew Dora would be nicking things.'

'You think our sneak thief is doing the same, Alf?' I put to him.

'Like father like son, like mother like daughter, it makes sense. That girl would grow up with aniseed around the house, she'd see her mum sucking it when she was moody and tense . . . I reckon she'd do the same. It's just a thought, Sarge, but it's funny the victims say they smelt something odd.'

'Well, PC Rhea, just in case PC Ventress is right, you had better arm yourself with a bag of aniseed balls and be sucking one as you return to see Mrs Littler. You can ask if that is the smell she noticed. Then perhaps a visit to Sheila Firthland? Even if she is guilty, I doubt if she will confess, there is very little evidence to connect her with the crimes and I doubt if a court would convict her on the smell of an aniseed ball.'

'She would leave fingerprints on the purses and bags she touched, and perhaps on the doors,' Alf pointed out.

'I doubt if we could get a suitable impression from the surface of a purse or handbag, or even a door knob,' said Craddock.

'She is not to know that,' smiled Alf.

'Perhaps you and PC Rhea should visit her, after talk-ing to the complainants about aniseed balls?' suggested Craddock.

'A good idea,' enthused Alf Ventress.

'So, tell me, PC Ventress,' continued Craddock, 'if the mother was investigated and prosecuted, we might still have records, might we?'

'Oh, yes, there was a very thick file on her, Sarge.'

'And where will it be now?'

'It was in the loft, Sarge. I hung on to it last time we had a clear-out. Sergeant Blaketon couldn't see the point of hanging on to the file because all the crimes had been committed such a long time earlier, but I craftily hung on to it. You never know, do you, when you're likely to need a file again? Criminal families and all that. We're talking of generations of breeding here, Sarge.'

'All right, I get the message. Can you find the file?'

'It was under Exploded Bombs, Sarge, so it's lying on the floor right behind you, among the stuff from the bomb file.'

Craddock blinked and looked at the ragged heap of files which were now spread across the floor after their unceremonious tumble from the loft. And there among them was 'Dora Minton, born 12 April 1916. Prosecuted for larceny from shops, Ashfordly. Northallerton Quarter Sessions, spring 1941. Sentenced to two months' imprisonment.' Inside were the relevant court papers, statements and details of the police investigation. Craddock picked it up.

'I find that amazing, PC Ventress, that this very file should land virtually at my feet after all this time, precisely as we are embarking on an associated enquiry. Coincidence is an odd thing, is it not?'

'Not really, Sarge. I heard Nick telling you about those crimes and thought we might need that file. I knew where it was and dropped it with the bombs.'

'Does that mean I am supposed to read some kind of message in all this?' Craddock frowned. 'Are you saying I should not throw out any old files, just in case they might be useful in the year 2000 and beyond?'

'I don't think we need worry too much about keeping files on stray dogs, Sarge, not those more than ten years old. The files, I mean, not the dogs . . .'

'Look, PC Rhea, get yourself down to the sweet shop in the market place, buy yourself some aniseed balls with the money I shall provide from official sources — and get a receipt — then both of you get along to have another word with those victims. If you feel you are on the right track, with the aniseed connection, then go on and interview the Firthland woman.'

'Right you are, Sarge,' beamed Alf.

'And brush your uniform, PC Ventress. Now, immediately, before the public sets eyes on you.'

We purchased quarter of a pound of aniseed balls in a white paper bag and took one each, but after sucking them for a while we had no idea whether or not we exuded an aroma. If only one of us had been testing the sweets, then we might have noticed a smell upon the other.

Nonetheless we presented ourselves to Sue Littler and then to Jilly Hartley and each confirmed that it was the scent they had noticed in their homes. We explained that we had a suspect although we did not, at this early stage, reveal the identity of our aniseed-sucking sneak thief. Instead, we made our way to No. 121 Lingmell Road, the home of Sheila Firthland. She opened the door to us — and she reeked of aniseed. Even after completing our sample, we could smell the aroma which enveloped her.

At first, she denied all knowledge of any thefts in the Limetree Grove area or any other part of Ashfordly, but when Alf said we would examine the handbags and purses of the two complainants with a view to finding fingerprints, she admitted her guilt. We then received a long sob story of how her husband had been out of work and there was no money in the house to feed and clothe her child; she had been compelled to steal from those she felt were better off than she. And when Alf suggested this might be an opportunity to

admit to any further crimes — to be 'taken into consideration' as the formal term described it — she provided a list of
more than a dozen houses she had raided — none of which
was then known to us.

'It was so easy,' she shrugged. 'Just walk along the backs
of those houses, see the purses and handbags in the kitchens,
check the woman is not around, hear her upstairs hoovering
or whatever, and dive in. It takes seconds to nick a few quid,
half of them never miss it. I always left a bit behind. I wasn't
greedy so long as I had enough for me and the bairn during
the week. And with me taking the bairn for a walk round
town, who'd suspect me? So how did you get on to me?'

I was about to offer her an aniseed ball, or to ask if she
stole to feed her habit of sucking them, when Alf cut me short
by saying, 'Let's put it down to good old-fashioned police
work,' he smiled. 'Sound detective techniques and a deep
knowledge of the town and its people.'

We did not arrest her because she had a child in bed
upstairs but told her she would be reported for summons in
due course. We visited the other houses to which she had
confessed visiting and some women had no idea their purses
had been raided, although some remembered noticing an
odd smell which had lingered for a while in their kitchens.

We returned to the police station feeling very pleased
with ourselves and I settled down to complete the necessary
paper work which always flowed from this kind of event.
One day, the file I was compiling would find its way into the
loft and I wondered if some future constable, when enquiries
into the behaviour of Sheila Firthland's child, would remember it and its association with aniseed balls.

Then Sergeant Craddock came through from his office
just as Alf was arriving with some mugs of tea he had brewed.

'Ah, PC Ventress. Pray tell me this: what are all those
dogs doing outside the police station? There must be at least
a dozen of them.'

'It's the aniseed, Sarge, they follow the scent. Now,
I have some uneaten aniseed balls and so does PC Rhea,

official constabulary issue of course, so shall I throw them to the dogs?'

'No you will not! I seem to recall that we have a police station boiler which is not doing a lot at the moment, so I suggest we dispose of them there. Unless you wish to consume the lot?'

'What, and have half the dogs of Ashfordly follow me? Not likely!'

And so Alf produced his surplus sweets and I did likewise, placing them in the palm of my hand. He said, 'Looking down upon these spherical objects, I could say something rude, but I won't.'

And he took them all to the boiler house, opened the lid and threw them in, then turned to me and asked, 'You don't think we should have kept them, do you?'

'I suppose we could have retained them in the file I've just opened, labelled as an exhibit, or just listed as "Modern Crime Investigation Techniques",' I smiled.

'They'd become a bit sticky after ten years in our loft,' he laughed. 'No, we did right. Good riddance I say.'

'Well, they did put us on the scent of the real culprit,' I added, and he groaned.

CHAPTER 10

During my time at Aidensfield, burglary was a very rare crime. The number of burglaries within the entire North Riding of Yorkshire was extremely low because it was a crime considered so serious and so rare that it equated with murder and rape. That arose because burglary could be committed only at night, i.e. between 9 p.m. and 6 a.m., and only at a private house; the law had been enacted to ensure that one's private house was as safe as the proverbial castle. Under Common Law, burglary carried the death penalty but when the Larceny Act of 1916 codified the crime, the penalty was reduced to a maximum of life imprisonment. Clearly, not many people took the risks associated with a prosecution for the crime of burglary.

The lesser crime of housebreaking (which could be committed at other times of the day) was much more prevalent, as were shop-breaking, garage-breaking, office-breaking, warehouse-breaking and so forth. Since 1968, however, all such illegal entries into buildings have been reclassified as burglary; the term now includes the entire range of 'breaking' offences, even that formerly known as sacrilege which applied to churches and other places of worship. Since that change in the law, the number of burglaries has increased beyond all recognition. No longer does it attract the death penalty nor even life imprisonment; today, the penalty is a maximum sentence of only fourteen years' imprisonment, a penalty rarely if ever imposed. It is not surprising, in view of all the changes and reduction in status, that burglary is now amongst the most common of crimes. We should be grateful that murders and rapes have not increased to the same degree.

In 1960s Aidensfield, burglary was so rare that my records did not reveal the last time it had occurred on my patch. There had been a few housebreakings and associated entries into properties like shops, garages and even green-houses, but those did not cause great concern. But one day, I received a report of burglary.

The call came from Mr Peter Barnes who lived with his wife, Rachel, in Moorcross Cottage, Thackerston. In their mid-60s, the couple had both retired, Peter — always known to his friends as Pop (Post Office Pete) — having worked for the post office at Ashfordly, latterly in a managerial capac-ity, while Rachel had been employed as a secretary at a local chemist's shop. They had a daughter, Ruth, who had moved away from home some years earlier but no other family; for some reason, Ruth never came home, and the Barnes did not talk about her. The couple were very quiet, decent and good-living even if Rachel was considered rather straight-laced and humourless. She would never do her washing on a Sunday, for example, and did not visit public houses, nor did she enjoy alcohol at home. She did not smoke, and the house lacked warmth; there was no pretty wallpaper, nice pictures on the walls, frilly curtains or even vases of flowers. It was austere and very plain inside.

Pop was certainly the more affable of the two and he did a lot of voluntary work for charities, while Rachel restricted her voluntary work to sick animals, cats in particular. Pop was not a churchgoer and so the church did not benefit from his efforts, and he once told me he preferred to 'commune with God on my own terms and in my own way, nothing

organized, no dressing up, or smells and bells'. Rachel, however, attended chapel in Elsinby; I don't think she was a true
Methodist because she did not partake in any of their events,
other than to attend on Sundays. But whatever her beliefs,
she sought sanctuary in Elsinby's curious wooden chapel
whenever convenient, yet steadfastly declined invitations to
join events like the Harvest Home or anniversary celebrations. Pop and Rachel preferred their own company, seldom
inviting anyone in for a meal, but their very sheltered life
caused no one any harm and if I had to call for any reason, I
was always made welcome.

It was with some surprise therefore, that I received a
phone call to say they had been burgled — with no antiques
in the place, and Rachel not given to wearing jewellery, I
wondered what on earth could have been stolen. But the
call came very early one Wednesday morning, around 7.15,
as I was climbing out of bed after working late the previous
evening. It was Pop.

'Can you come, Nick?' he panted into his telephone.
'We've been burgled.'

'Is he still there?'

'No, no sign of him, he'll be well away. I've just discovered it.'

'Give me fifteen minutes,' I said.

I rang Ashfordly Police Station and caught Phil Bellamy
who was working early turn, spending the first part of his
shift in the office.

'I'm going to a reported burglary,' I told him. 'At
Thackerston, not known yet what's been stolen. Radio all
mobiles, Phil, there might be somebody hitchhiking who's
worth a check, some vehicle racing away . . . you know the
sort of thing.'

'You'll call when you've more?' he asked. 'Like a description of the stolen goods?'

'I will,' I promised and hurried out of the house.

Moorcross Cottage was a long, low single-storey building on the side of the main road which swept down through

Thackerston in a series of smooth curves. The cottage had been converted from a series of outbuildings which had once been part of Moorcross Farm. The land had been sold off and the farmhouse was now a large and opulent private house owned by a businessman from Leeds; Pop and Rachel had fashioned the conversion into their modest home. I parked my van and went to the front door, but Pop had observed my arrival and the door was opened even before I reached it.

'So where did they get in?' was my first question after I had listened to a more detailed version of the raid.

'I've a study at the back, a little room I use for myself. I'll show you,' and Pop led me along the rear passage into a small square and rather dark. room. It had a Yorkshire sliding window which was standing open, but there was no sign of broken glass.

'He opened that window,' Pop said. 'I haven't touched it since. He must have put something between the frame to lift the catch; it's easy enough. A knife blade, I imagine. And all you have to do is push the window aside.'

'It's not very secure!' I remarked, noticing there was no damage to the woodwork. But a slim blade could easily be thrust between the window frames.

'Well, no, but we've never had trouble like this before,' he said. 'Nobody ever breaks in around here, not at night anyway.'

'Well, my first recommendation is to screw down all your windows or get locks for them. So after sliding the catch off, he eased that window aside and climbed in; we're on the ground floor so that would be no problem.'

I studied the window sill inside the room but there were no footprints; outside was a grassy area and I thought some mud or other debris might have been brought inside by the intruder. But the night had been dry and the window sill and floor inside bore no such marks. Then I looked at the rest of his study — this man was a serious stamp collector. The walls, shelves, desk and all available surfaces provided evidence of his hobby; posters, pictures, maps, catalogues and albums lay around, with lots of loose stamps scattered across his desk.

'I see you've a big collection of stamps?' I put to Pop.

'I've been collecting since I was at school,' he said with pride. 'These are all mine, gathered from around the world . . . it helped, working for the post office . . .'

'And the thief ignored them?' The indications were that nothing had been touched in this room.

'Obviously he's not a stamp collector,' he smiled ruefully. 'A good job, really, I've got some very valuable ones.'

'So the first you knew was when you came in here and saw the open window?'

'Yes, that would be about half past six this morning. I felt the draught. I had closed it last night, I'm sure of that. I checked it before going to bed. I always do.'

'What time was that?' I asked.

'Half past ten or so. Early to bed and early to rise, that's me. Up before six; it's a legacy from my post office days.'

'And when you came in here this morning, the culprit was nowhere to be seen?'

He shook his head. 'No. I had a look round — I took my gun with me, I might add, the twelve bore, just in case!'

'So where did he go from here?'

'Into the kitchen I think, because some money has gone. It's next door to the study.'

'Show me.'

We stepped out of the study into the rear passage and at the end, on the left, was the kitchen. He led the way, saying, 'Rachel keeps her spare cash in a biscuit tin on the mantelshelf, for the butcher when he calls, the insurance man and so on. It's gone, the tin lid was off which is why I noticed it, and the tin is empty.'

'How much has gone?' I asked. I was in the kitchen by this time and saw the tall, rounded biscuit tin with a lid beside it. I did not touch it but looked inside. It was empty, with not even a stray coin remaining.

'You'd have to ask Rachel. I haven't much idea, some-where about five pounds or so I'd guess. But she's not here, she's staying with her sister in Harrogate for a few days. Her sister's a widow, you see, and they used to be close as girls . . . Rachel likes Harrogate.'

'And has anything else gone from the kitchen?' As I looked around there was absolutely no sign of any distur-bance. It did not seem that a search had been made.

He smiled. 'An apple, I think. I'd set my breakfast table before going to bed, I always do that, and I put an apple beside my side plate. It's gone!'

'An apple.' I had to smile. 'I'm not sure how to value that. So, cash and an apple stolen from the kitchen. Did he leave then, do you think?'

'No, he went upstairs, into the spare bedroom. There's no sign of anything being touched in the lounge or dining room. No drawers opened; we've a silver tea service, a wed-ding present, and that's still there. Now upstairs, we've only the one spare room, right at the top of the stairs. The drawers have been searched, but we had nothing there, no jewellery or anything, and I don't think anything's been taken.'

'I'd better have a look at the whole house.'

I examined every downstairs room and agreed with Pop that the intruder had not searched them or stolen anything from the ground-floor rooms, other than the cash and the apple. He led me upstairs to the spare bedroom and that did have all the indications of a frantic search. Decorative boxes opened on the dressing-table, but their contents were untouched, talcum powder spilled, drawers pulled out and their contents — spare sheets, pillow cases, some clothing and women's underwear — strewn all over the floor. The wardrobe doors were standing open too and it was clear the pockets of some men's suits had been searched while the woman's clothing had been dragged out on to the floor. There was a box of letters on the floor, with most of the letters tipped out.

'I didn't touch anything,' Pop told me ruefully. I learned not to, working at the post office. We had rules to follow if any of our premises were entered.'

'That's good, Pop; you'd be surprised how many house-breaking victims have an urge to tidy up and dust before the police arrive! That's the worst thing they can do, they destroy lots of valuable evidence. So what was among those letters?'

'Nothing so far as I know, just letters. Rachel tends to keep family correspondence,' Pop said. 'That box is usually in the bottom of the wardrobe.'

'So what's he been looking for? Jewellery? More cash? Valuables of some kind?'

'I have no idea, we're not rich people, Nick, we have no valuables of that kind. Rachel isn't one for wearing jewellery. Those decorative boxes were used for trinkets, knick-knacks and they've not been stolen, as you can see. It looks like a hurried search to me, but why that room? Why not empty the sideboard downstairs and take our china or cutlery?'

'And this is the only spare bedroom?'

'Yes, I was in the other one.'

'Was any attempt made to enter your room, do you think?'

'Well, I doubt it. I do snore a lot, so Rachel tells me, and I guess the intruder would not come in if he knew I was there. I'm sure he must have heard me and crept away . . . my theory, for what it's worth.'

'So did you hear anything during the night, Pop?'

'Not a sound. I'm not deaf, but I am a little hard of hearing; it goes with getting older, you know, and I sleep very soundly. Rachel says it would take a bomb to wake me once I nod off!'

'So he did not take anything from your bedroom?'

'No, nothing, nor the bathroom, or anywhere else.'

Having chatted with Pop and then made a second, more detailed search of the house, along with the loft and garage, just in case chummy was still hiding on the premises, I concluded he had made good his escape — with only a few pounds in cash and an apple. It seemed very odd, very odd indeed.

'We will need to know if there was anything of value in that spare room, Pop, so have you told your wife?' I asked.

'No, not yet, it's still early. I don't really want to upset her. She's having a nice relaxed few days with her sister. It's hardly worth ringing her, not for a bit of cash and an apple.'

'There could be more. It does seem that spare room was the focus of his attention, Pop. It's almost as if it was deliberately targeted. So let's consider what might have been there, something you did not know about. A handbag full of cash, savings for a rainy day, perhaps? Bits of spare cash tucked away from the housekeeping, that sort of thing. Something Rachel might have kept secret from you?'

'But even if Rachel had done that, who would know about it?' he asked.

'Professional thieves know that people do conceal spare cash, especially pensioners, and they know where to look for it,' I told him. 'Wherever cash is hidden, a professional thief will find it. Or it could be someone who might have used that room in the past. Has anyone used it recently?'

He shook his head. 'No, it used to be my daughter's, Ruth's. When she was living at home. She was our daughter.'

'Was?' I caught the use of the past tense.

'She went away to work, in Manchester, as a personnel officer in one of the big stores. She never married.'

'And presumably she uses this room when she comes home?'

His eyes misted over. 'No, Nick, she died in a traffic accident. Six years ago. We've accepted it, the room is not a shrine to her, nothing like that. We're sensible about it. If Rachel's sister comes, the one from Harrogate, she will use the room, but it's hardly used otherwise. No one else has slept there.'

'I'm sorry, Pop, I had no idea. Nobody's mentioned that to me.'

'We rarely talk about it,' he admitted.

I took a deep breath, for I had to continue. 'So we do not know for certain if anything has gone from that room, and that raises the question: why would anyone want to break in to your house at night, search that room and yet take away only a few pounds in loose change and an apple?'

'You tell me!' he said. 'Maybe he thought we had jewellery or, as you say, some hidden cash . . .'

'If he'd wanted valuables, he could have taken your stamp collection, or part of it,' I said. 'That's the first thing he would see on gaining entry, and he could have taken that without going into any other part of the house. In my view, Pop, this thief has been searching for something in particular. And that means we must contact your wife, to ask if she kept anything in that bedroom.'

'She'll be so upset, and frightened. She might not want to sleep in the house after this.'

'Very few houses are burgled a second time,' I tried to reassure him. 'Now, how do you think he left the premises? I presume your front and back doors were locked?'

'Yes, but both have Yale locks. He could easily open either door from the inside and slip out.'

'Right; now I must have a look around the outside, to see if there are any footprints in the garden or other signs.'

'Shall I put the kettle on? I could do with a coffee!' he said. 'It's been quite a morning.'

'Yes, you do that. I'll make a tour of the exterior, then I'll have to report this to my sergeant. I'll contact him by radio from my van while I'm outside. He might call out the Scenes of Crime Officers, to see if they can find fingerprints or other evidence. You have to be very careful what you touch before they've been, and I need you to make another complete check of your belongings, just to make sure nothing else has gone.'

He said he understood.

I continued, 'The fact he took cash and an apple suggests a hungry and hard-up traveller of some kind. I've already circulated a message asking for all hitchhikers and such to be stopped, interviewed and searched. But if he's got away with only an apple and some cash, we'll have difficulty proving he took them from here! And I bet the apple's gone by now!'

'I'll put the kettle on while you're doing that,' he smiled.

'Don't touch anything else in the kitchen,' I warned him. 'Use cups from somewhere that's clearly not been touched by our intruder, like that sideboard in the dining room. But you understand that, from your post office days.'

'Right,' he said.

Feeling rather like Sherlock Holmes, I made a careful tour of the exterior as I stared at the ground to see whether chummy had left any evidence of his presence. Separating the garden from the road was a low stone wall. Moorcross Cottage had two gates, one leading along a concrete drive to the garage, the door of which was closed and locked, and a smaller hand gate leading along a narrower concrete path to the front door. The front of the house comprised an extensive lawn, neatly cut, with well-tended borders all around, now full of flowers and shrubs. A path ran to the rear where there was more lawn close to the house and a vegetable garden further behind. I found nothing; even when I looked at the study window from the outside, there were no marks on the ground and none on the window frame. The window had not been forced, but I could see that the blade of a pocket-knife could easily be slipped between the two sections of the Yorkshire sliding window frame to lift the catch. The window could then be opened from the outside. Whoever had done this had not left a single mark or clue.

However, when I went through the hand gate and on to the road, I did find something. The area between the wall and the road comprised a neat grass verge, about four feet wide, but between it and the wall there was a narrow strip of cultivated ground, bearing flowers — currently, it was full of pansies — and I found a mark in the soil — it was a cycle tyre mark, the front wheel I felt because the mark was angled. I didn't think a rear wheel would have left a such a mark so close to the wall. So had a bicycle been leant against this wall? If so, had it belonged to the thief? The mark was obviously recent — the definition was sharp; it had not been weathered. Currently, there was sufficient tread mark for a plaster cast to be made, and for that to be compared with any cycle tyre we might later discover. A raid by a passing cyclist? Someone short of cash and hungry too? It was feasible, but had it been an opportunist crime, or had it been planned? And if he'd been hungry, why not take more food?

Before returning to the house I radioed Ashfordly Police Station and by this time, Sergeant Craddock had materialised in the office. Phil Bellamy handed my call to him. Craddock listened intently then asked, 'You call this a burglary, PC Rhea. Are you sure it is a burglary? I feel inclined to record it as a housebreaking. Much better for our crime figures, you understand.'

'Mr Barnes checked the window at half past ten last night, Sergeant, and it was secure then. And he discovered the illegal entry at half past six this morning.'

'So entry could have been made between six this morning, and half past six this morning, could it not?'

'He was out of bed before six, Sergeant, knocking about the house.'

'But even so, he did not discover the entry until half past six. That makes it housebreaking, PC Rhea. We do not know for certain that entry occurred before six, that is most important. I do not want an undetected burglary on my returns.'

'I can have another chat with Mr Barnes, but I am sure the intruder was not in the house when he got up. He must have entered after ten last night and before six this morning!'

'But we cannot be sure, can we? Even if he does get up early, he discovered the break at half past six this morning; even if we know the window was shut at half past ten last night, the crime should be recorded as a housebreaking. Housebreaking it is, PC Rhea. I have my crime figures to consider. So, tell me more.'

I briefed him on all the circumstances, making due reference to the cycle tyre mark, and he decided that Scenes of

Crime Officers should be called to examine the house and its surroundings, and to take a plaster cast of the tyre mark.

'If we find a cyclist, PC Rhea, and if his tyre matches the mark you have found, it does not prove he committed the crime, but it does place him very close to the scene. And then we can take his fingerprints and with a bit of good police work — and some good luck — we might find matching prints inside the house.'

'Right, Sergeant.'

'You will radio SOCO and await their arrival, will you?'

'I might make a few house-to-house enquiries nearby, Sergeant, while I am waiting. Someone might have seen something, and people will be out of bed by now.'

'Good thinking, PC Rhea. I may decide to visit the scene too.'

Those necessities took me about fifteen minutes or so, and when I returned Pop had a couple of Coronation mugs prepared, and some biscuits he had found. As I explained what I had done, he made the coffee and then said, 'While you were out there, Nick, I rang Rachel at Harrogate. She's devastated, as you can imagine, and said she might stay a while longer with her sister. She's very upset that someone has rifled Ruth's room . . . but she said there was nothing of value there. No jewellery, no heirlooms, nothing like that, only spare linen and clothes, and those letters. No secret hoards of cash either.'

'OK, thanks for that, but I must tell you that sometimes property is not missed until a considerable time afterwards. When your wife comes home, perhaps she would make a thorough search and let us know if anything has gone? Thieves have been known to take clothing, scarves, gloves, even shoes!'

'Yes, I'll do that but after chatting to her, I'm sure nothing's been taken.'

I enjoyed the tea and biscuits, then told him I would make a few enquiries from the near neighbours as I awaited the arrival of SOCO. As they had another job, they'd be here in about an hour, I told him. He said he would settle down for his breakfast, after asking me what I thought he could safely touch.

Occupants of the first few houses at which I called could not help, but when I called at Thackerston Grange, the farmer, Don Fairclough, said, 'We had a visitor last night, Mr Rhea. A young lass on a bike, touring the area, she said.'

I felt a tingle of anticipation as I obtained a description of the cyclist — he said she was about seventeen, fairly tall, with a slim figure and dark hair, and she had a south of England accent. She had been dressed in cycling clothes, with long black trousers, or tights, and a bright red shirt. Her bike, a lady's model with a pale-blue frame and straight handle-bars, of the touring type, had twin panniers on the rear in which, she carried her belongings. Across the top of the pan-niers, she'd had a rolled-up sleeping bag and her waterproofs.

'We're lambing,' he told me. 'I had to get up early, half-five or so, and found her asleep in the haybarn. We had no idea she was there; then she woke up and apologised for not asking permission. She said she'd arrived late last night and didn't want to disturb us, so she just crept in and went to sleep in her sleeping bag. I told her to stay as long as she wanted this morning; we have an outside toilet with a tap and I said she could use that. Anyway, when I looked in again about half-six, she'd gone.'

'Did she give any idea where she was going?'

'No, just touring the area.' He tried to recollect his con-versation with her. 'We had a bit of a chat, just a bit. She said she'd come to York by train, with her bike, from King's Cross last night, and was touring this part of Yorkshire. She'd been before, she said, and knew her way about, but was too late to get fixed up in a youth hostel or such. She never said where she'd come from or how long she would be here, or where she was going when she left us.'

I thanked Don and asked him to ring me if he saw her again, then decided I should return to Moorcross Cottage to await SOCO. They hadn't arrived, and I asked Pop if he had seen the girl on the bike, but he shook his head. 'She never called here, not to my knowledge.' He shrugged his shoulders. 'But a girl wouldn't break into a house, would she?'

'Why not?' I put to him. 'Girls commit other crimes!'

'Well, I can't imagine a young girl would do a thing like that . . . anyway, while you were away, I've had second thoughts,' he said unexpectedly. 'That money that was missing . . . I might have taken it.'

'You?' I asked.

'I went to the shop yesterday, I had to pay the paper bill and get some groceries, things Rachel had asked me to see to, so I think I took that money because I'd given most of mine to Rachel for her trip. My memory isn't what it was you know, short term I mean. I can remember things I did when I was a lad, but sometimes can't recall what I did the day before . . . so I might have taken the cash from that biscuit tin. I wouldn't want somebody punished for something they never did . . .'

'If there is any doubt at all,' I told him, 'I can't include it in my list of stolen items.'

'I think we'd better forget that bit,' he blushed. 'Sorry. So now I'm wondering if the burglar came into the kitchen.'

'The apple, you mean?'

'I usually put one out beside my plate, ready for breakfast, but when I went for one just now, when you were out, they were all there. Those I bought yesterday — six apples. So I don't think the thief took one. I think my memory's going.'

'But the room, the spare bedroom?' I had to ask. 'That was visited, wasn't it? There's no mistake about that, is there? Rachel would never leave it like that, I'm sure, and you've not been searching for something, have you?'

'Somebody's been in there, Nick, definitely, there's no doubt about that . . .'

'And the window? You did close it last night?'

'Yes, I did,' he said. 'Yes, definitely. I do my rounds before I go to bed and I checked it; it was closed with the latch down, like I said, before I went to bed. At half past ten.'

'You're absolutely sure?'

'I am,' he said firmly.

I must admit I was now having doubts. I began to wonder whether there had been a raid at all, or whether it was all in Pop's imagination, but before I could call Ashfordly Police with details of my suspect for them to circulate, SOCO arrived. Detective Sergeant Stan Browning and Detective Constable Alec Cresswell comprised the team and I briefed them, albeit not at that stage voicing my doubts about Pop. After a look at the interior, I led them to the cycle tyre mark in the outside border.

'We've a suspect,' I said, describing the girl on the bike. 'I'm going to call Ashfordly now, to circulate a description.'

'We saw her!' said Browning. 'On the road between here and Galtreford.'

'When?' I almost barked at them.

'Oh, an hour ago. We had a job in Galtreford, before coming here.'

'Which way was she going?' I demanded. 'Where was she exactly?'

'Going towards York,' he said. 'Walking up Winter Hill.'

'I'm going to look for her,' I said.

'She's had too much start, she could be anywhere,' said Browning.

'She came from York, last night, she might be heading back this morning,' I said. 'I'll radio the railway police at York to look out for her; they might come across her if I'm too late.'

It is difficult to know why I felt she was heading back to York to catch a train to London with her cycle on board, but after speaking to Pop, I felt his story about the raid did not ring true. And that feeling had been aggravated by his claim that he might have been mistaken about the stolen cash and missing apple. There was a mystery here — I could sense it — but I could not determine its nature.

Beyond doubt, however, was the fact that a girl on a bike was somehow involved and she had been seen heading for York only a short while ago. Pop had changed his story when he discovered I knew about the girl; he'd reacted to my suggestion that a girl might commit such a crime, and he'd come up with the tale that he might have been wrong about the cash and the apple. So did he know the girl?

There were many unanswered questions and I felt the cyclist could answer some of them. Even if she was innocent, she had to be found and questioned. And quickly! I was the person to do it, so I radioed Ashfordly, contacted Phil Bellamy and explained what I was about to do, and asked him to telephone York railway police to look out for the girl on the bike and to detain her for questioning. I did not want her to catch a train and escape before I had chance to talk to her. I left SOCO to conduct their examination of the scene.

I arrived on the concourse at York's famous railway station just as a uniformed railway policeman was intercepting the girl. Her description matched that given to me by Don Fairclough and, as I approached in my uniform, the railway policeman noticed me. The girl was standing nearby, holding on to her bike and looking utterly miserable, and somewhat frightened by this unexpected development.

'I'm PC Rhea from Aidensfield,' I identified myself to the constable. 'My office will have called you?'

'Marshall, British Transport,' he said. 'And this, it seems, is the young lady in question.'

'What do you want?' she began to blurt out the words. 'Who are you? Why are you doing this to me?'

'I've had a report of a burglary at Thackerston,' I said. 'I'd like to talk to you about it.'

'I didn't steal anything!' Her eyes revealed her terror now. This was no professional thief — I could see she lacked the toughness. This was a frightened girl.

Marshall said, 'Let's go into the office, we can talk there. Bring your bike.'

'My train goes soon . . .'

'If you don't talk to us, you'll be going nowhere,' he said, and I must admit I did not like his threatening attitude, mild though it was. 'Come along.'

He led us into the police office at the side of the concourse and showed us into an interview room, complete with table and chairs. He asked a policewoman to join us and the girl's cycle was left in the passage. 'She's yours, PC Rhea,' said Marshall.

We invited the girl to sit on the chair at the table while Marshall and the policewoman stood near the door; I sat on the chair opposite the girl. Although she looked adult, it was policy to have a woman present while interviewing all females.

'What's your name?' I began.

'Margaret Barnes,' she said.

'Barnes?' This surprised me and for a moment I did not know what to ask next.

Then she surprised me by volunteering this: 'I am seventeen, and I go to school in South Norwood. I have a flat in a house belonging to the parents of some friends, and I work part-time in a bookshop to earn some pocket money. I have no father and my mother is dead, I get a share of her pension being next of kin,' and she then gave her date of birth and her address. Was this a show of defiance or misplaced confidence? She seemed streetwise — a London trait for a young woman perhaps?

'You know Peter Barnes of Thackerston?' I asked.

'He's my grandfather,' she said, maintaining her defiant attitude.

'So you are Ruth's daughter?' I spoke softly now.

'Yes, and you will know she is dead.'

'Yes, I'm sorry. Look, Margaret, something odd is going on and I am not party to it, so I am going to ask you to be honest and open with me.'

'I did not steal anything!' she snapped. 'You said something about a burglary.'

'I was called to the scene of a burglary, a break-in at Moorcross Cottage during the night, or in the early hours of this morning. Some cash was reported missing, and an apple, and one of the bedrooms was ransacked.'

'Is that what he told you? That I had broken in and stolen things? He said he was my friend . . .'

'No, he did not say you had done it. We heard you had been in the area, at the farm overnight. We had no idea you were his granddaughter. He doesn't know we have found you, Margaret, so I think I had better hear your side of the story, don't you?'

'I got into the house, through a back window. It wasn't locked, the catch was not on and it was easy to slide it open. It was early this morning, before six. He gets up early and he caught me.'

'What were you doing?' I decided to adopt a gentle approach.

'Looking for this.' She opened the top of her cycling blouse to reveal around her neck a beautiful silver necklet bearing a handsome pendant set with diamonds. It looked to be early Victorian and she removed it, handing it to me. There was a monogram on the back of the brooch; I could discern the letters E.G.

'Who is E.G.?' I asked.

'My great grandmother,' she said. 'My grandmother's mother.'

'So, why break into your grandparents' house in the early hours of the morning to steal this necklet?'

She then told us the story. Her mother, Ruth, had become pregnant with Margaret but was unmarried at the time. The man responsible had vanished and had not been seen since. Ruth was left to bring up her child. However, Rachel Barnes was very old-fashioned and bigoted, Puritanical in fact, so far as sexual morals were concerned, and she had rejected Ruth, saying she wanted nothing more to do with her. Ruth had left home to earn her own living and to bring up her child — she had never returned to her parental home and had died tragically as the result of a traffic accident six years ago. As Margaret grew up, she had learned something of her background from her mother, and later from her great aunt, Esther, who lived at Harrogate. Mother and daughter had often stayed with Esther, for Esther had always shown kindness to them. From those family chats, Margaret had learned about this necklet — it was passed down through the family on the female side at birth — and so, claimed Margaret, it should have been given to her upon her birth, but it had remained in Ruth's bedroom. Granny Rachel had refused to hand it over to her illegitimate granddaughter.

'Great Aunt Esther was more like a granny to me than my real granny,' Margaret told me. 'When Mum died, Granny Rachel came to the funeral, the first time I had seen her. I was eleven, but I knew about the necklet, and so I asked her if I could have it. She refused; she wouldn't even talk to me or discuss it. She said I must never try to visit her or contact her. She said I had inherited Ruth's shame.'

'What a rotten thing to say!'

'I was upset, Mr Rhea, very upset and hurt. I'd done nothing wrong, but Great Aunt Esther said the necklet was rightly mine and she told me where it was, so I decided, long ago, that I would get it by whatever means I could. I knew Granny Rachel was at Harrogate this weekend, at Great Aunt Esther's, and I knew Grandad would be alone, and that he was a bit deaf . . . I didn't want to visit him to ask for the necklet, as that wouldn't have been fair on him. I'd looked around the house before, once or twice, when they were out. I'd been there before, you see, to Thackerston, without them knowing. With my bike. I was trying to see where I came from, I suppose, where Mum had been born, and so I knew about that loose back window . . .'

'It was not latched?' I asked.

'No, it never was. He was very careless; in London he'd have had nothing left by now! Anyway, I came up from London yesterday with my bike, slept in a hay byre and this morning set about getting my necklet. I slid back the window and got in, and I was searching the bedroom when my grandfather came in with his gun.' And here she paused a moment.

'Go on,' I invited.

'I thought he was going to shoot me. He thought I was a burglar. I shouted it was Margaret and I'd just come for the necklet . . . he flopped on to the bed and took me in his arms, saying he'd always wanted to be friends, but Granny would never hear of it . . . we had a good cry and he helped me look for it. Then he said I should take it and go, and he would pretend a real burglar had been, so Granny would never know I'd got the necklet. We messed up the room, I think he enjoyed that . . . then we had a cup of tea in the kitchen and he gave me some money and an apple and said I should get as far away as I could.'

'On your bike?'

'Yes, he said he'd wait for a while then ring the police and report the burglary, to cover his tracks, so she'd never know I'd got my necklet . . . he's frightened of Granny I think . . .'

'I think you had better come back to Thackerston with me,' I suggested. 'We can put your bike in the back of my van, and I want you to tell this story to my sergeant. I think we should get this supposed crime written off.'

'You won't tell Granny Rachel, will you? I don't want to get Grandad into bother.'

'That explains the money and apple,' I smiled. 'But I think you should try and make friends with your grandmother.'

'She won't hear of it. She shuts her mind. She thinks she's a Christian . . . she's no Christian, shutting me out like that . . . but Great Aunt Esther is nice, I see her a lot.'

'Come along, Margaret,' I said. 'Let's get back to Thackerston.'

'I nearly got away, didn't I?' she grinned suddenly. 'I was nearly a successful criminal!'

'You were very amateurish,' I said. 'You left far too many clues at the scene, and your collaborator did not tell a very believable story. But come along, young lady, you and your grandparents have a little sorting out to do.'

I delivered Margaret to her grandfather who said she could stay in the room they had trashed — and she would clean it up. Pop admitted he had not telephoned his wife to check for stolen items, for it was his idea to make her believe, on her return, that burglars had been responsible and had taken the pendant. He'd thought the tale about the apple and cash would add to the story! The offence of wasting police time had not then been created and it was felt the circumstances did not justify prosecution for compounding a felony; instead, Pop received a written caution from the superintendent.

The incident was written off as 'No Crime' much to Sergeant Craddock's delight, but as I left Pop and his granddaughter together, I wondered how a man could be so afraid of his supposedly Christian wife as to deny the reality of his family.

Margaret left Moorcross Cottage before Rachel returned from Harrogate and I left the explanations for Pop to deal with. But Margaret did now have a family — or half of one! She and her grandfather kept in touch, but Rachel refused to accept the girl into the house.

THE END

ALSO BY NICHOLAS RHEA

Thank you for reading this book.

If you enjoyed it please leave feedback on Amazon or Goodreads, and if there is anything we missed or you have a question about, then please get in touch. We appreciate you choosing our book.

Founded in 2014 in Shoreditch, London, we at Joffe Books pride ourselves on our history of innovative publishing. We were thrilled to be shortlisted for Independent Publisher of the Year at the British Book Awards.

www.joffebooks.com

We're very grateful to eagle-eyed readers who take the time to contact us. Please send any errors you find to corrections@joffebooks.com. We'll get them fixed ASAP.

Printed in Great Britain
by Amazon